THE LIFE THAT NEVER ENDS:

AN ANTHOLOGY

OF QUAKER SPIRITUAL/PSYCHIC EXPERIENCE

Quaker Fellowship for Afterlife Studies
www. quakerfellowshipforafterlifestudies.co.uk.
2019.

Published 2019

Printed by
Leiston Press
Masterlord Industrial Estate
Leiston
Suffolk
IP16 4JD

ISBN: 978-1-911311-54-6

Copyright © QFAS

Cover design by Rebecca Lee
Photograph of a Norwegian fjord by Tina Day

All rights reserved. No part of this book may be reproduced, stored in a retrieval system, or transmitted in any form or by any means electronic, mechanical, photocopying, recording or otherwise, without prior permission of the author.

CONTENTS

ACKNOWLEDGEMENTS   ii

FOREWORD   iii

INTRODUCTION   1

SECTION HEADINGS

1.	As death approaches	9
2.	After death communications	16
3.	Near death experiences	53
4.	Animals and the afterlife	64
5.	A miscellany of spiritual experience and comment	71
6.	Experiences of Early Quakers	120

SUGGESTIONS FOR FURTHER READING, etc.   129

ACKNOWLEDGEMENTS

The Committee of Quaker Fellowship for Afterlife Studies is grateful for two donations which have enabled the printing of this book. The first is a grant from the Joseph Rowntree Reform Trust, the second is a donation from the family of John Noble, given in his memory. John, who died in December, 2018, attended Heswall Quaker Meeting for many years and was a committed Quaker and long standing member of QFAS.

We are also grateful to all those Friends who have contributed accounts of their experiences and made this Anthology possible.

The title of this Anthology is taken from the writings of William Penn, and dates from 1693, (Quaker Faith & Practice, 22.95, 1995.) The full quotation is given on page 120.

FOREWORD

... Are you open to new light, from whatever source it may come? Do you approach new ideas with discernment?

Advices and queries: 7

Many years ago when I had been a Quaker attender for only a short while, I was sitting in Meeting one day and became aware of a very large lady who seemed to be standing directly in front of one of the other people there. She was what we would now term as obese, dressed entirely in black and with grey hair in an untidy and shapeless bun at the back of her head. What was very noticeable was the fact that the old-fashioned hair-pins were constantly falling from this bun and landing on the floor. And what is very noticeable now is the clarity with which I can remember her, although I have hardly any impression of the person she was with. And that person obviously had no indication that she was there, even though the lady herself seemed agitated and keen to be acknowledged. My feeling was that this was a motherly figure, either her mother or grandmother. The constant dropping of the hair-pins was accompanied by an awareness that this was a permanent feature of this lady which would serve to make her recognisable.

I spent the rest of the Meeting wondering if I dared to mention this afterwards, but was too unsure of the reception I would get. And this is our problem within the Society of Friends and particularly in Meeting, which is the very place most conducive to extra-sensory perception. We relax and open ourselves to the Spirit, make ourselves ready to receive inspiration and yet so often when there is some insight given to us, or some spiritual message or awareness of otherness, we are too afraid to give voice to it; too afraid of ridicule and rejection.

In the first instance *we* need to rise above this fear and give *ourselves* permission to speak, and in the second many of us need to relinquish any judgement on those who, by faithfully recounting their spiritual and psychic experiences, can shed light on, and bring some understanding about, life beyond its merely physical manifestation.

So this Anthology gives 'permission' to many Quakers to admit that many of us can and do receive spiritual and psychic intimations. We are not just bodies but also souls, or psychic beings, the word 'psyche' meaning 'soul'. We need to surmount our fear and suspicion and acknowledge that 'there are more things in Heaven and Earth... than are dreamt of in your philosophy' (*Hamlet, Act 1, scene 5*).

(And I must confess I never did mention the lady with the falling hair-pins!)

At the time of going to print the clerk of QFAS is Angela Howard, Webb's Cottage, Woolpits Rd, Saling, Braintree, Essex, CM7 5DZ. Email: angela1@webbscottage.co.uk. If you would like to discuss any experiences you may have had or have any queries we may be able to help with, please make contact.

Rosalind Smith

INTRODUCTION

*"We are not human beings on a spiritual journey.
We are spiritual beings on a human journey."*
authorship unknown *

In July 2000, a group of six Friends met at Claridge House to discern whether to proceed with the formation of a Quaker After-Life Studies Group. Two members, Angela Howard and Rosalind Smith, had recently published booklets on the subject, and the response to these indicated that many Friends thought the subject important. Furthermore, and worryingly, they felt that it was not a matter which they could easily raise with other Friends in their Meetings. Accordingly, a major lack, which QFAS was founded to remedy, was the provision of help and support for people with psychic gifts and experiences within the Quaker movement (providing a forum for discussion and learning, and exploring evidence for the survival of death, being the other part of the Group's remit).

By the end of the Claridge House meeting the fledgling group had decided on a limited set of objectives to be achieved during the following year. The first Anthology, entitled *The Unfamiliar Country: Communication Beyond Death, An Anthology of Quaker Spiritual/Psychic Experience* (2001), was one of our early projects. Gradually we made contact with like-minded Friends, and the stories, hitherto largely kept private, began to unfold.

This first Anthology was succeeded in 2006 by a second edition, enlarged by a section on the spiritual experiences of early Quakers, written and compiled by David Britton. In between, one of the founder members, David Hodges, authored *Do We Survive Death? A descriptive bibliography and discussion on the evidence supporting survival* (2004), a significant achievement, now out of print.

Within a few years the Quaker Fellowship for Afterlife Studies became a Listed Interest Group of Britain Yearly Meeting (since 2017 it has become

---

*This quotation is often attributed to Teilhard de Chardin but this is thought to be inaccurate.

a Quaker Recognised Body), with a newsletter, an annual day conference at Friends' House, and an autumn weekend residential conference at different locations around England. These conferences were well attended and much appreciated. Membership of QFAS has always been around 150 – 200.

Over the years, members have written books, and articles for The Friend and other Quaker periodicals, and links with like-minded groups such as the Churches' Fellowship for Psychical and Spiritual Studies and the Unitarian Society for Psychical Studies have developed. Two joint conferences have been held with these organisations.

Writing now in 2019, a pattern of annual weekend residential conferences at Woodbrooke has been established as part of the Woodbrooke programme. Every other year the conferences are held jointly with Friends' Fellowship of Healing; QFAS has closer links with FFH than with any other Quaker group.

The day conferences at Friends' House, though popular, have had to be dropped as there is currently no-one able to organize them. However, special interest group meetings held annually at Britain Yearly Meeting are well attended.

In 2010, when QFAS had been in existence for ten years, the committee put out a statement:

QFAS' first Woodbrooke Conference this year, was entitled "The Afterlife: How good is the evidence?" The answer, we decided, is: "very good indeed. And very empowering."

One cannot continue to look at evidence for ever. Sooner or later a verdict has to be reached. So the committee agree that the time has come to move on, and in the next ten years of the life of QFAS to take our "verdict" to a wider audience with confidence and fresh energy.

The reason for this, of course, is to help people overcome the debilitating fear of death! Knowledge about life beyond death can bring comfort and reassurance to those approaching their own death or that of family members; and for younger people it can bring a new sense of meaning and purpose, once physical life is seen as part of a greater whole. We believe that the existence of life beyond death is a truth, and that an understanding of this truth is part of our birthright, and not something which should remain hidden.

Belief in an afterlife is linked to no particular religion. We believe that a large body of overwhelming evidence has accumulated over many years clearly indicating the survival of the human personality. One day we hope that the strength of this evidence will be widely accepted.

But don't take our word for any of this! The only way forward is to set out on your own voyage of discovery and see where it leads you.

The Religious Society of Friends, since it is a religious society, should have no problem with the discussion and upholding of spiritual experience. Such experiences can constitute a vision every bit as radical as any outer-directed activism. Meeting for Worship itself puts the notion of the possibility of expanding consciousness right at the core of Quakerism.

We wish we could say that Friends can now confidently and safely raise these matters within their local Quaker meetings and other Quaker gatherings, and that providing a supportive safe exploratory space for Friends is no longer needed so much. Unfortunately, this is not the case. Over the years many sad stories have been told, by members and those who contact the Fellowship, of the lack of understanding of and interest in spiritual/psychic experiences too often found in Quaker Meetings. We hear frequently of encountering the 'glazed look', even hostility, when such subjects are raised with other Friends. This situation within the *Religious* Society of Friends is one which needs to change urgently.

Our present-day western culture is shaped by a scientific materialism which often seeks to ridicule and crush anything which cannot be reproduced in a laboratory experiment, or measured with the tools currently available to it. Along with humanism, it asserts that there is nothing guiding our destinies greater than human intelligence, and no meaning to the world other than that which we give it. Any other point of view is considered weird and outdated, and many Christian denominations have also been unsympathetic to spiritual experience which stands in some way beyond the boundaries of their own theologies. Something of these scepticisms has permeated much modern British Quakerism, obscuring the fact that Quakerism was founded on an unequivocal belief in a real encounter with the Divine.

But there has always been a current of thought which has resisted materialism. In recent decades it has been seen in an important and growing swell of books, on-line talks and interviews, coming from deep thinkers, scientists, doctors, academics, which questions the paradigms of scientific materialism and humanism. Phenomena such as Out of the Body and Near Death Experience provide evidence for consciousness as a non-local energy. The implications of this are enormous and so it is not surprising that the resistance to these things is huge.

This is the cultural context that partly explains why people who have spiritual experiences do not feel safe to speak about them. Over the past 20 years the Society of Friends has allowed this wider sceptical context to permeate a place where faith in things unseen or inexplicable should be upheld. Doubt is a normal part of the individual spiritual life, but the Society has permitted the institutionalization of doubt, and facilitated outright denial of any extra-material dimension to life. This is why it is so necessary that anthologies such as this should be compiled. The greatest comfort and support for someone with an unusual personal experience is to be able to share it and find they are not mocked and not alone.

What do we mean by 'spiritual'? One meaning of the word gives it an ethical focus: the spiritual person is a *good* person, a person who is trying to pursue a life of selfless service to others, and to avoid causing hurt. This is a meaning which most humanists could agree with. It is enshrined in that form of Christianity which remains when its supernatural components are removed: Christ as the earthly revolutionary and supremely good man, not the Son of God. If we are only human beings on a spiritual journey, perhaps ethical behaviour is a major definer of that journey. In Quaker terms, this makes the notion of 'that of God in everyone' mean only that there is in people the possibility of awakened conscience, of altruism, of the highest ethical behaviour and self-sacrifice. It becomes a moral proposition.

But this anthology is concerned with a bigger meaning for the word 'spiritual' – the use of the word to refer to realms of experience which go beyond the boundaries of our usual perception in some way, that cause a significant shift in our sense of who and what we are, what the world is, and what lies beyond the world. And if we are spiritual beings on a human journey then in some fundamental way we are already a part of this vast spiritual dimension. Then 'that of God in everyone' becomes a metaphysical statement, not just a moral one. There is 'that of God in everyone' regardless of whether they are in touch with it or not, and regardless of whether they are capable of acting ethically. Quite a different thing.

Spiritual experiences can be light and fleeting, through many degrees of strength, to long and intense. These experiences are often deeply meaningful and they are often about connection between people, and can initiate profound life changes: from synchronicities, to intuitions, the sensing of energy or presences, dream encounters, states of oneness and ego-loss, angelic meetings, and glimpses of other dimensions.

The descriptions and stories you will read tell of interaction, often fleeting and only partially apprehended and understood, between life in the physical world, and life in another dimension, a dimension beyond time and space as we understand them; a dimension which seems to encompass and contain and give deeper meaning to our material existence.

These experiences, which come unbidden and are beyond the realm of our familiar five senses, vary enormously. They may be words from a departed loved one, a sight of that person, a familiar scent discovered in a closed room, a dream. They may involve pre-cognition, as when the traveller hears the inner voice which warns "Don't travel on that plane!" They may seem to come from a higher source and be an intimation of a particular line of action we should follow. They may come to us directly, or through an intermediary, a medium, sensitive or psychic.

The noun 'psychic' is often used in a derogatory way to describe someone claiming a paranormal gift (or simply an intention to make money and fame by pretending to have one). They operate, or purport to operate, in the world of communication beyond the five senses, but often it is only when they are mistaken or are discovered to be outright frauds that they come to our attention through the media. Bad news is easier and quicker to relay than good, and sells faster! The careful, sensitive work that psychics often do, particularly in helping the bereaved, is usually overlooked or ridiculed. For those who receive a message which seems to be a clear contact, the joy and sense of reassurance is indescribable.

'Psychic' in the sense we use it in QFAS denotes a level of contact with the unseen world which is personal and based on love and need. The contacts come from those close to the earth plane, and belong more to the world of the everyday. 'Spiritual' guidance seems to come from a higher level, from guides of various kinds or guardian angels; some might even say from God. It depends on the terminology with which we are familiar. There is much which is uncertain about how this is achieved. But the message, the feeling, the guidance, however it comes, feels right and good and stays with us. Those who have experiences of contact with the unseen world of whatever nature, usually never forget them. They are precious in a way we find difficult to explain.

Also included in this Anthology, are some examples of 'Out of Body Experiences' (OBEs) and 'Near Death Experiences' (NDEs), the "I was suddenly lifted up out of myself" events often at moments of trauma, and peak experiences of a never-to-be-forgotten sense of otherness and bliss; a sense of enlargement and revelation such as has been described by contemplatives and mystics through the ages.

We hope the reader will enjoy and discover that which elucidates or confirms their own experience, and that which brings them possibilities both new and amazing. All the contributors are members of the Society of Friends, or regular attenders of a Local Quaker Meeting. In a few cases the stories have been told to Quakers by those known personally to them. They have been collected over the past twenty years and most have appeared in our newsletters and journals. We are grateful for all of them. We apologise for any omissions and ask for forgiveness. Sifting and selection has been an enormous and sometimes daunting task!

Remember that these selections are only a tiny part of the totality of such recorded accounts which have been published beyond the Society of Friends. There is much more to explore if these stories whet your curiosity and appetite. May the words in this book bring enlightenment, hope and comfort to all who are struggling towards greater understanding and also in overcoming doubt. It is our intention in publishing to make known that which is of vital importance but often kept private. It is our gift to the Society of Friends and to the wider world.

QFAS members
September, 2019

21.54

Death is not an end, but a beginning. It is but an incident in the 'life of the ages', which is God's gift to us now. It is the escape of the spirit from its old limitations and its freeing for a larger and more glorious career. We stand around the grave, and as we take our last, lingering look, too often our thoughts are there; and we return to the desolate home feeling that all that made life lovely has been left behind on the bleak hillside… Yet the spirit now is free, and the unseen angel at our side points upwards from the grave and whispers, 'He is not here, but is risen'. The dear one returns with us to our home, ready and able, as never before, to comfort, encourage, and beckon us onward.

William Littleboy, 1917

21.56

I believe it is of real value to our earthly life to have the next life in mind, because if we shut it out of our thoughts we are starving part of our spiritual nature – we are like children who fail to grow up – none the finer children for that. Not only do we miss much joy in the earthly life if we imagine it to be the whole of our existence, but we arrive on the further shore with no knowledge of the language of the new country where we shall find ourselves unfitted for the larger life of the spirit. George Fox urged Friends to 'take care of God's glory'. That is a motto for all spheres known and unknown.

Joan Mary Fry, 1955

(Quaker Faith & Practice, 1995.)

1. AS DEATH APPROACHES

When death is approaching as part of a natural, unfolding process, there is often an awareness on the part of the dying person that family and friends who have already passed on are gathering to welcome, give reassurance and help carry them over. There may be a sense that the dying person is partly in this world and partly in the next, moving gently between the two. Those close to the dying person in this world - family, friends, nurses - may also witness these events.

My grandfather died shortly before his 95th birthday at our home where, at the time, we were bringing up our three young children. He had joined us for a large family Christmas party but contracted pleurisy from which, despite the best of care, he did not recover. He was a retired Welsh Congregational minister - still preaching by invitation in his final year - and a man of unwavering faith, joy, great wit and humour.

On the last day of his life he insisted on being helped out of bed so that he could sit in a chair and smoke his pipe and, at that point, he said quite calmly, 'Well, I'm off. I'm leaving you tonight' - and he did!

After getting back into bed he slipped into intermittent sleep or coma but did not speak again until late into the night. Then, quite suddenly, he lifted his head and turned it towards a side door leading to the bathroom, exclaiming loudly and with delight, with a radiant smile of recognition on his face, 'Annie!' Whether in reality or imagination he was undoubtedly seeing and greeting his late wife - calling her by his "young" name for her rather than the customary "Mama" which he had consistently used after the arrival of his children. (My grandmother, who had suffered from Alzheimer's disease for many years before her own death twenty years earlier, had not been referred to during my grandfather's final illness.)

For those of us who witnessed it, it was an incredibly moving and inspiring moment and we were left convinced that, as is reported in so many "near death" experiences, my grandmother had somehow come to "meet" him at the moment of his death in order to "hold the hand of a stranger in Paradise" (to paraphrase the old song!) That experience proves nothing, of course, but it remains a treasured, powerful and encouraging memory for those of us who shared in it.

Jill Inskip

Many years ago an elderly Friend in the late stages of dementia who liked the Silence in our Meetings for Worship gave most moving ministry. Her son who had no particular religious affiliation would drop her off at Meeting. She recognised nobody although I visited her at home. Shortly after Meeting for Worship had started Mary became noisy and restless. This was totally unusual. Friends seemed embarrassed and did not know what to do.

Sitting in the back row of the Meeting I got up with my two walking sticks, needed because of Multiple Sclerosis, shuffled to where Mary was and as the seat beside her was empty I sat down and put my arms around her. We remained like this for the next half hour. She became very quiet; then Meeting became 'centred' and seemed to enter a deep place - a real sanctuary.

Shortly after, Mary started to speak, just a few words or sentences now and then. It was as if she was carrying on a conversation with someone very special but we could only hear part of it. No-one interrupted. Her ministry was accepted by the Meeting and it was as if we were all accompanying her in silent prayer. 'The Light is wonderful.' 'How kind of you to come.' 'Yes, all is well.' 'I am not afraid.' This was part of what we heard her say.

About five minutes before Meeting ended she cried out, 'Jesus, please wait. I'm coming too. Don't leave me!' 'Oh, he's gone. I am alone again.' This was her last time in Meeting. She passed over peacefully in her sleep a few days later. At the Meeting for Worship for Mary at the crematorium, her "ministry" was shared by another elderly Friend. It made a big impression on many and her family especially were very moved by it and were greatly comforted.

Isobel Bracewell

The call came from the hospital to come now. This was easier said than done because we live on an island with a drive of over 250 miles to reach my mother's bedside. The journey through Skye felt very slow, tourists were everywhere and preferring to travel slowly. I made the best time ever, despite the delays.

Needing to have a break I pulled off the road at Glengarry where there is a beautiful small car park amidst the forest beside a swiftly flowing stream with mountains all around. Before pouring coffee from the flask, I phoned my husband to tell him where I was. There was a long silence. Quietly he said, 'I have something to tell you', so I knew before being told that my mother had died. She had died before I even left the ferry. 'There is no rush now', John said, 'take your time. Go for a walk, take as long as you need and please go carefully'.

I sat with the coffee watching a small bird; he didn't know that mother had died. Another car drew up, four young people got out, laughing and running off in the opposite direction. They didn't know that mother had died. After a while I got out of the car and started to wander down a small path beside the river. My legs seemed unable to carry me. My answer to most things is 'go for a walk', but this time walking was difficult. There were boulders almost in the rushing water.

There I sat. I tried to make my mind go blank, watching the water streaming by, the eddies and the flows. As I watched, the river was transformed into a lake, still and quiet. The trees were no longer the conifers of the northwest highlands but deciduous trees. I noticed a large oak. There was a path along the opposite bank. As I watched there were two young people laughing and holding hands. Sometimes they ran, sometimes stopped to watch something. They were very happy. The girl had long thick brown hair hanging in curls far down her back. She wore a summer dress, with a brown and pink flower print. The lad had his hair parted in the centre and stuck down with grease of some sort. They both looked vaguely familiar, I wondered, was I sure? Was this my mother and father in their youth? What was I seeing?

Then the vision, for that was what it was, faded and I was once more sitting on a boulder beside a highland river. I was left with an overwhelming sense of peace and, almost, Joy. How could I admit to this?

Later that evening I spoke to my aunt, my father's younger sister, with whom I had a close relationship. I described what I had seen. She laughed and said that I was describing the Hollow Pond in Epping Forest with my mother and father as teenagers. It had been a haunt of theirs. The dress had been my mother's favourite and it used to irritate my aunt that my father used lard to stick his curly hair to his head. My aunt was so pleased with the vision. I described the sense of peace and even the joy. Of course, said my beloved aunt, this was your mother sending you a clear message that she and Jack were together again and that they are happy. I was glad of that message of comfort that my mother sent to me.

That evening my daughter was sitting by my side. She said that she had had a vivid dream, only she did not think that she had been sleeping. She had seen my mother sitting under a large oak tree surrounded by all the much loved family dogs including her own beloved Jet, who had died. My daughter said that my mother was very happy with all these dogs around her; she was playing with them and smiling. There can be no doubt that my mother had found peace and joy immediately after her death and she wanted to reassure those who loved her of this. Her spirit was very alive and well.

Robin Goodman

My mother, Grace, died on her birthday. My father, Rex, had died 15 years earlier.

On that day of her birthday, Grace was gradually becoming sleepier. But, she knew it was her birthday and that soon all the family would be gathered around her bed for the special teatime. Her 4 month old grandson had just visited for a cuddle, but had now gone for a sleep. My younger brother and I were sitting on either side of her bed, holding a hand each. Suddenly, Grace looked up, and gave a big beaming smile of welcome, whilst joyfully saying my father's name - 'Rex'. His spirit had evidently arrived in order to escort Grace to the Afterlife. Neither my brother nor I were aware of his presence. My mother then released her hands from ours, holding out her arms in the same direction she had smiled her greeting. She then stopped breathing and died.

Elizabeth M Angas

Mag was my father's sister and she and I were very close. As Mag became older we had conversations about death and what might happen. On one of these occasions she asked me to be there with her when she died. I answered that with 600 miles and the Minch between us I could not make such a promise but I did promise to do my very best to be there. Her response was, 'Oh well, in that case I will wait for you'. When the call came from the hospital, I was on the first plane the next morning, hoping that she would wait for me. Sitting on the plane, I was aware of my father. I could not see him but he told me that he was off to meet Mag.

Mag did wait for me and died very peacefully, holding my hand, a few hours after I arrived. I believe that I saw her soul fly away over the fields that she loved so well. I also believe that my father, her beloved brother was there to meet her.

Robin Goodman

About a month before she died, my eighty-three year old Mother was in hospital following a serious operation. She was asleep when I arrived to visit her so I sat quietly by the bedside watching her closely and waiting. Suddenly she stirred and moved her head to one side as if she had been touched on the cheek. Then a smile spread over her face. A few minutes later she woke and, sounding pleased and surprised, said, 'Someone just kissed me'. 'I know,' I said. 'It wasn't me, but I saw it happen'.

Angela Howard

Towards the end of my husband, Joe's, life, he was confined to a bed downstairs, spending most of his time asleep under the influence of his medications. I found that by being still and going into a state of mindfulness, I could link to him which was a way of checking on him when I was not in the room, or was even out of the house.

After a few days, I became aware of a presence standing in my room. At first it was a shadow figure. The room was filled with a sense of peace and love... I knew it was Joe.

I practised this technique from other places in the house and garden, and eventually when out, and could always "feel" if I was needed or all was well. Soon I began to sense this even when not trying, perhaps sitting reading, or working in the garden. I became aware that each time I saw him there was a glowing light round him. This started as a small amount round his feet, increasing gradually until the light slowly covered him to his neck. This was over a period of 5 months. Never was there any feeling of distress from this figure or indeed anywhere in the house.

During the second week of July, Joe always appeared completely in the glowing light which now surrounded his whole body, becoming more lovely every day. Eventually he was just a "Being of Light".

On 20th July Joe went into Spirit, not having spoken or seemingly been aware of the nurses or myself for about a week. I felt sadness at the loss of his physical presence, but also joy at knowing that he was now free after a long illness.

Doreen Varley

Wherever you are, I'll be there
Whatever you say, it won't be wrong,
I'll be listening to your heart far more than the words.
Whatever you do, I'll be radiating love
Whatever you want, I want it for you
Whatever you choose, I'll be happy for you
Don't worry, be happy.

I know you will be sad, but don't be too sad
I want you to live, and enjoy the living
I want you to love, and play, and be joyful
I want you to be happy,
I want you to remember that nothing matters.

Matter is illusion
Time is illusion
Death is the biggest illusion of all.
I'll be with you when you need me
I'll be somewhere having fun when you don't.
Be compassionate, to yourself and others
Be honest, especially to yourself
And I'll see you soon.

Fee Berry

2. AFTER-DEATH COMMUNICATIONS

The number of contributions in this section is an indication of the greatest area of interest in spiritual/psychic experience for QFAS members. From the days when the Fellowship began, Friends have had an intense wish to share stories of after death contacts with loved ones which, for the most part, they had felt unable to speak about for fear of ridicule. When these experiences were actually invited, the flood gates opened!

The contacts described come in many forms. Mostly they are what might be described as mental contacts, coming through the mind of the bereaved person in some way. A few, which may be more difficult to explain, concern actual physical effects on electrical or mechanical devices in the home.

Those who do not receive contacts sometimes feel the lack of them, and perhaps ask themselves if their love was not strong enough to survive death. This does not seem at all to be the case; it is more likely that other circumstances such as intense grief (which we are told causes a psychic block) may play a part. Sometimes an intermediary with mediumistic gifts may be needed to create the link.

In my experience there are a number of ways in which contact can be made with those who have died. The subtlest are fleeting perceptions of the person which are sensed by a kind of receptive inner vision. These perceptions resemble becoming aware of what is on the periphery of normal vision, except no image is seen with the eye; it is only an inner vision. The deceased sometimes manifest some distinctive look or gesture, with an accompanying expression of delight and freedom. There is usually a strong flavour of the personality. These images can sometimes occur when in a calm and reflective mood, thinking about the deceased. They can also happen if you are doing something which makes a connection to the person – such as visiting their home. They are quite delicate and so easily missed, or if of a sceptical turn of mind, dismissed.

In sleep our consciousness opens and can be receptive to external influences. Dead friends can enter a living person's dreams and conversations can take place which will be recalled in part on waking. These experiences differentiate themselves from standard dreams by the sense of the reality of the other person and sometimes by the depth of positive emotion which is shared. I would compare the strength of emotion after one of these to waking after one of the earliest happy evenings out with a person you have just fallen in love with and who loves you also.

I had one about a university friend who seemingly committed suicide by a drug overdose. While asleep I found myself in a comfortable but unremarkable furnished lounge sitting opposite her. She appeared as I remembered her from the late 1970s. We had a conversation in which she described what happened. She described lying on a bed and finding herself having an out-of-body experience, and being surprised by what was happening. It was clear from what she said that she was not in her right mind when she took the overdose of anti-depressants and therefore the suicide was not entirely intended. I had been thinking about her for some weeks before this happened as I was writing a piece of music in her memory. I believe that type of deep focus is what enables contact to be made because it can be picked up from the other side. A friend of mine had one of these a day or so after a friend of his was killed in a car crash.

At the other extreme there is the materialisation which makes the deceased visible to ordinary vision, in broad daylight, and capable of seeming physical contact. One of the friends of C. S. Lewis had this experience with Lewis a few days after his death. I know two people who have had this happen to them. One was a woman in her sixties whose husband appeared about 7 years after his death and kissed her. I believe this happened then because her grief had lifted enough to make it possible. I think intense grief can create a block to these subtler contacts.

The other example is a woman who was a WAAF during World War II and lost her fiancé in the Battle of Britain. She was haunted by this trauma all her life and then after 50 years was persuaded to write down her memories.

It was then that her fiancé appeared to her, again in apparently physical form. Over 50 years had elapsed since his death, which reminds us that time in the after-life runs at a different manner/ rate to this life.

Rikky Rooksby

Marjatta Bryan sent the following account, following the death of her husband Alex. It was written by a member of her Meeting who saw Alex at his funeral service on 5th May 2004.

On the morning of Alex's funeral I spent some time contemplating his life. I had first met Alex at Winchmore Hill Meeting in 1996. He was a shy and deep-thinking man and on the few occasions when he ministered, his ministry spoke to me. Alex was a conscientious objector during the war and had written books about this period in his life. These stories spoke to me deeply.

When Alex started having difficulty with walking, it was my great pleasure to take Alex and Marjatta by car to Meeting on Sundays, and our friendship deepened. Alex was a man with great depth of feeling and it made a great impact on me.

Over the years I saw Alex's health deteriorate and what inspired me was the way he always held onto his dignity, never complaining, and with great courage. Towards the end of his life Alex was confined to hospital on more than one occasion and I had the privilege to visit him a few times. On my last visit before he died, I realised God was calling him home. For one moment he opened his eyes and there I met those most beautiful eyes, a mirror to the soul.

When Alex's funeral at the crematorium was in progress, I felt a deep sense of connection with him. God's presence was all around me and I knew that God was holding Alex in his arms. Time stood still until I was moved to minister.

My ministry concerned our friendship and the love I had for Alex and the hope that Alex would hear the words God had spoken, 'Today you will be with me in paradise.' After the ministry I felt a great joy of inner light and peace and I passed this to Alex in my thoughts. As I looked at his coffin, I found him sitting on the catafalque and asked him in astonishment: 'What are you doing there, Alex?' He did not look at me; he was engrossed in reading a book. He looked young, vibrant and well and I realised he had returned to his youth. Light was all around me; it was as if all the fireworks that had ever been made had been set alight all at once. Alex rose from the catafalque and walked to the left and then to the right around the coffin. His hair was dark and he wore a white shirt. My greatest joy came when I noticed his grey trousers. He was walking unaided, tall and straight, with no sign of the problems he had encountered during his earthly life.

Peace and gentleness prevailed and this was his farewell message to us. Alex had become glorious in his faithfulness. The flowering of his spirit lives on as a light to each one of us with memories of him. I love him dearly, and maybe his gift to us is to love one another as God loves us.

Linda Davis

An experience occurred after the death of a friend who was a fellow musician. One evening I sat grieving, and struggling to write about my feelings. Suddenly I heard her well-known tones, telling me not to be silly; of course she was all right, and it was nonsense to make such a fuss. It was as if I felt her spirit travelling by me like the wind.

A similar experience happened after the death of another friend, whose husband also was very close to my husband and myself. On the morning of her funeral, I started the day in quiet, and I then heard her ask me to give a message to her husband: 'Tell him it's all right, and I am on my journey.' I did as she asked, and heard afterwards that it had comforted her family. Of my most important and extended experience, I cannot give a full account here; but I must mention it. Some years ago, someone with whom I had been out of touch for thirty years came to tell me that he had died. We talked together; and there followed a series of frequent conversations over several years. In the end this intimacy came to a natural close. I can't here briefly convey the quality of this relationship, though I have tried to do so in my sequence of poems, *Borderland*.

Joan Benner

From my teens onwards I had experiences of telepathy, and occasionally of clairvoyance; however, I knew nothing of communication with the dead until I was in my forties.

I saw my father only once after he died. It would be two or three months after the event; I was standing at the dressing table twisting my hair into plaits. It was mid-morning, a bright clear day in early summer and I caught sight of him through the window behind the mirror. He was walking up the path by the garage, dusting off his hands as if he had been pulling a few weeds.

I remember looking down and noting the dusty patch on the right knee and thinking that my mother would be telling him yet again he should change into old trousers if he was going to be gardening. But then, lifting the odd weed is hardly gardening, is it?

He turned the corner between the garage and the coalhouse and disappeared from my view. It was only when I had finished doing my hair and had tied the ribbons on my plaits that I realized why I had not heard him come in by the kitchen door. I could not understand how I had forgotten he was dead.

I come from a family with a Highland mother who were not at all surprised by such sightings but our inlaws were not all so accepting. One of my sisters, home with her relatively new husband, was visiting Mother. To his dismay, she came into the drawing room with a tea tray and said, "I've just seen Dad standing at the foot of the stairs". He later told my brother he could feel the hair standing up on the back of his neck but when Mother barely glanced up from her sewing and answered, "Och yes. He's always hanging about there", poor George wondered what kind of family he had married into!

Muriel Robertson

My father died in hospital in the week between Christmas and New Year, and my mother was too incapacitated to be with him. She received the phone call from the hospital at about 6 am after spending the night alone except for her old cat who always slept peacefully at the end of her bed. Suddenly, while she was still holding the phone, the elderly moggie began to career around the room, trying to climb the walls, seemingly out of his wits. Obviously he was seeing or sensing my father's presence.

A day later, in the evening, while I was staying with Mum, there came a phone call from a very old friend of Dad's – they had been in the army together. He asked to speak with Dad and when I told him he had died the day before there was silence at the end of the line. Eventually he said, 'Well, I haven't thought about him for about 15/20 years, but he's been in my mind all day today'.

I said, 'Perhaps he's come to let you know he's still around!' More stunned silence at the end of the phone – then I wished him the season's greetings! Dad had gone back to a friend of about 50 years previously, which seems to show that time is irrelevant over there.

Rosalind Smith

My father died 1st January 1960. The first time I was aware of his presence was a year and a half later. I was rather poorly in early pregnancy and my mother was severely disapproving to the point where the doctor had advised my husband to keep her away from me. One day, lying in bed, I became aware of my father's presence. He was sitting on the armchair in the room with his feet up on the wall and he was wearing a Fair Isle sleeveless jumper that my mother had knitted for him. He told me not to be worried or upset, that both the baby and I were going to be alright and that my mother would come round and be pleased with her grandchild.

Dad still comes on occasions, although I have never *seen* him again, just have a comforting knowledge that he is there. He watches over us, and my grandson, at a time of great distress, saw a person who was a good presence. When my daughter described the person Peter had seen, it was undoubtedly my Dad.

Robin Goodman

Over the last few years six F/friends have contacted me on the third or fourth day after their deaths... haven't we heard this before somewhere? Two Friends just dropped by, one saying, ' I seemed to have gone over' and another asking me to give her love to a Friend, but one, Dinah, a Friend who was an elder at my AM, has come a number of times in a very supportive way... once an elder always an elder!

She encouraged me to attend the last QFAS conference at Woodbrooke and urged me to report it at AM and if I was bold enough, to give her love to Friends...I was and did but you can imagine the reaction - about three faces lit up with interest the rest could only be described as stony.

One day last year a neighbour dropped in. He happened to say he was feeling very low as it was two years since his partner had died. The next day she came to me and asked me to give him a message... to let him know that she was always with him and helping him and that if he spoke to her she would hear him. I thought I cannot do this he'll think I'm nuts, so I procrastinated. She came three times and asked again and again. He happened to telephone so I took the opportunity to tell him... he responded with, 'Oh you're one of those are you'? Who knows whether he believed me or not?

She came the next day and thanked me.

A difficult encounter was with someone whom I considered to be a good friend and whom I'd known a long while. Her husband came to me on a number of occasions asking me to go and see her. He wanted to thank her for looking after him and to give his love and pass on the knowledge that there was more to life than we perceive on the material plane.

So one Sunday after Meeting when I'd spent much of the hour holding her in the Light, I called in on my way home. It seemed to me the right time. I was not prepared for the negative explosion that greeted me... so full of fury aimed at her husband and also at me for my audacity. All I could do was remove myself from this blast. She called around a few weeks later. I suppose she was extremely embarrassed at her outburst but rather than apologizing, she said that she couldn't believe that I could be so insensitive as to call when I did. If I hadn't gone I would've been letting her husband down - damned if I did and damned if I didn't. Who said, 'don't shoot the messenger'?

I do feel very privileged to have been given this gift but one hurdle I have to get over is that I might be considered a madwoman. A friend asked why I cared? Well because I want to be believed, of course. Clearly I need some lessons in tact, and to gain a bit more sensitivity to the feelings of those who are bereaved but it's hard for a plain speaking Quaker just wanting to impart the truth! I do understand that one needs to know to whom one can talk about the afterlife...we are all at different stages of development of spiritual awareness, but when one has been asked to pass on a message one just has to do it.

On a more encouraging note – 'You were right. It's wonderful. Keep up the good work and help Friends realise that they have nothing to fear.' These are the words communicated to me recently by Marion, a sceptical Friend, four days after her death.

I have to say that I'm conscious of the loving help and support I receive from my spirit guide and my soul mates. And so grateful for the existence of QFAS as there have been times when I really have questioned my sanity.

Pat Gundrey

A well-loved elderly member of our Meeting died suddenly. I was one of two in the Meeting whom he called his 'girlfriends' and we were both very fond of him. The service at the crematorium was held on the Friday and I attended, but Jenni was prevented. On the Saturday morning she 'phoned me to ask for healing as she couldn't settle down to her studies and felt very restless. After the healing session we were sitting quietly when she suddenly said: 'Oh! Leslie's here.' In her mind she immediately thought he must have a message for his widow but he said to her, 'Don't worry about Erica. She will be alright.' Leslie was jumping up and down with joy and said he was well and happy, and we were conscious of being surrounded by a great feeling of love. It seemed that he wanted to let us know that he was very happy. After the incident we decided that I would tell his widow about this when it seemed appropriate, which I was able to do a few weeks later, and it brought her great comfort.

Ruth C Martin

Recently our 105 year old Quaker friend, Olive, died. She had still been living on her own but latterly, only this last few months, with some carer help. She had only stopped her music teaching work at 99. One of her reasons for independent living was that she liked to play her piano at 11 at night and in her own detached house was able to do it.

Two nights before her funeral my husband and I were sitting eating our very silent supper in a room with door closed and curtains drawn. It felt particularly silent when suddenly I heard three separate and rather disparate musical notes, pleasant and not related to any instrument or tune. In no way was it like sounds from the phone so I looked at my husband and said, 'What was all that about then?' and then just got on with my supper.

On the day of her funeral I went first to my yoga class where I joked that all our phones were bugged nowadays and told them of the three notes.

During our Friend's memorial meeting in the afternoon there was of course much mention of our Friend's musical activities and at last I made the connection! So when the Meeting was finished I went over to someone who I thought was Olive's granddaughter to tell her about the 3 notes. She and her 3 companions became very excited, repeatedly asking me when I had heard the three notes. It transpired that while they were sitting there waiting for the meeting to start they had heard 3 notes, looked at each other and all said to each other that their mobiles were switched off, and then said that it was Olive telling them she was with them.

And, no, I did not hear the notes when they did; Olive would have felt she had already done her job with me I think.

Mary Hawker

My husband, Gerry, died suddenly and unexpectedly on 23rd December 2008 at the age of 54. On 15th February 2009, at about 8.00 am, I was lying in bed, between sleeping and waking (it was a Sunday). Gerry was standing, leaning on the window-sill, looking out into the garden. I was confused. In my mind's eye I could see the coffin in the grave, and I said, 'How did you escape from the grave?' Without turning to look at me (I was on his left side) he said, 'Oh! I've come too soon. I should have waited longer!'

At this I felt terrified that he would disappear, and my mind was racing, taking on board that he had died, but was somehow here now. I quickly said, 'It's all right. I'm catching up, I'm catching up!' Gerry then said, 'I've got a new body.' I looked, and saw that his body was perfect, opalescent white. It had a kind of sheen. I understood then that he had come to show me that he was all right.

When he died, his body had been horribly bruised due to internal bleeding caused by his condition, aplastic anaemia. Since his death I had been worrying about him and thinking of him in his damaged body. On one occasion, before he appeared to me, I had had the distinct impression that he was telling me he was not in that state any more, but it was wonderful to see him in his new body. Some of the time when we were talking, it was very fast, as though thought transference was taking place between us. After a while I dozed a bit, but when I woke I knew it had happened and remembered every detail of our encounter in a way that I am never able to remember dreams.

Jane Clist

One day in 1972 we went to Suffolk to visit a friend, Elizabeth, whose mother had recently died. As we came up the drive of her large Georgian house, I saw Elizabeth in the conservatory sitting in a deck-chair, shelling peas, and she waved as we drove past. We parked the car and, with our three children, walked around to meet her. We chatted, wandered through the garden for a while and then went into the house for lunch.

In the evening as we were driving home, John (aged 10) asked, 'Why didn't Mrs Owles have lunch with us?' I explained that she had died a little while ago and he said, 'But I saw her in the conservatory sitting next to Elizabeth!' Jenny (aged 12) said, 'I saw someone else sitting there, too. I thought it was a neighbour who'd come to see Elizabeth.'

I should explain that John and I had stayed a few days with our friend and her mother about a month previously, so that he knew Mrs. Owles quite well. Jenny had not visited the house before, though she was well acquainted with Elizabeth who often came to see us. She herself was quite overcome when I told her what the children had said, though she did add, 'Why couldn't I see her?'

Beryl Spence

As a student, many years ago, I had a strange experience. I was reading French at what was then, University College, Nottingham. Halfway through my course, both my parents died, my father first, my mother nine months later. I was devastated. The only way I could deal with my sorrow was by working harder than ever. As finals approached I would spend as much as twelve hours a day revising. One night, before an examination, I had a very vivid dream. In it, I had a pile of notes in front of me, but, try as I might, I could not make sense of them. As I awoke, I heard a voice saying, 'Ta mere n'est pas loin de toi.' ('Your mother is not far away from you'). I felt amazingly reassured. I sailed easily through the examinations and achieved a very good degree.

In addition to the comforting presence of my mother, I had also the awareness of the "voice". For me, it raises the question of the possibility of a guardian angel. Whose voice was it? Was it someone who had been with me throughout my childhood and school-days, learning French alongside me? How can it be explained?

Jessie Baston

When my father died we were staying with friends in France. My brother rang in the middle of the night to tell me about his death. I was very sad and remembered how depressed he had been after a stroke a few months previously, and how angry I had been with him for what I saw as the selfish way he had been treating my mother.

As I lay thinking about him I suddenly "saw" him. He was grey-looking and seemed to be intertwined with other grey-looking people: static and despairing. Then the scene changed and I "saw" him painfully toiling up an incline: a sort of defile, like a railway cutting with grey slab walls and floor!

I felt a huge jolt of compassion and knew I must help him. It came to me that I must pick him up in my arms like a baby and carry him up the defile. This I was able to do and when we came to the top I "saw" a beautiful, shimmering sea of light, which made me think of Debussy's music. I set him gently down and left him there, knowing he would have the strength to move forward on his spiritual journey, unhampered by the fear he had felt when he died.

I was so grateful to have been blessed by that experience; for the way my anger had melted clean away and for the loving closeness I had felt with my father during the vision.

Anthea Lee

When my Father died 30 years ago, I accidentally (in grief and absent-mindedness) touched the live wires on the garden mower and thought that was it! Suddenly I was strongly aware of my Father saying/thinking 'how can I help?', and I was propelled forward from the step I was sitting on – breaking the current. I was left with burnt hands only.

Then at my Mother's death, and the scattering of her ashes, her childhood friend came with us and brought primroses and violets to put into the ground. Out of deference to Aunt Mollie's feelings I was inclined to agree. But my Mother spoke so strongly from another plane, reminding me that all creation should be respected, and to put the flowers in water, that I concurred. Both the happenings were unexpected but so definite – I will never forget them.

It seems that when we are at our lowest or sublimely happy, we are in touch with that Inner Voice, a source of Power and Love.

Deep Peace of the Running wave to you.
Deep Peace of the Flowing Air to you.
Deep Peace of the Quiet Earth to you.
Deep Peace of the Shining Stars to you.
Deep Peace of the Son of Peace to you.

(Celtic Benediction)

Gill Sephton

A few days before my husband Jim's funeral I had a visit from a friend who had been close to him for many years. Whilst we were talking about Jim, the lights suddenly fused. My friend traced the problem to the summerhouse where some years earlier he had fixed shelving for Jim's large collection of books. Jim used the summerhouse as a place to write.

For some weeks I continued to have many problems with the lighting in our home – problems that couldn't be accounted for. In desperation one evening I was joined by Angela Howard and, having lit a candle, we spoke to Jim telling him everything was safe, he had no need to worry about anything and we asked him to solve the problems with the lighting. From that time onward the lighting problems ceased.

Sylvia Izzard

After the death of my husband, Ernie, I was aware of phenomena in the house. I saw hazy shadows and movement out of the corner of my eye. The light bulbs were fluctuating and I was having to replace blown bulbs frequently but I knew that there was no problem with the electricity. It only happened in the living room and kitchen, and only in the room that I was in at the time. Several times in shops the till would malfunction and once when a cashier had been rude to me, her till just closed down as she finished serving me and she had to be moved to another desk as the technician could not get it working again.

That was the first time I really laughed. I knew that Ernie was there protecting me. Shop alarms would go off as I walked out which I found really amusing. At Christmas time I had arranged for Ernie's name to be put on a tree of remembrance in the church at Rye and I went there to visit. On this occasion the alarm went off as I walked into a shop.

Eileen Farrah Jones

My mother, Margaret, died in 2002. We had always been close especially so in the years since my dad's death in 1993. We spoke regularly on the phone and from my childhood had shared an uncanny ability to "tune in" to each other's thoughts and moods even though latterly we lived miles apart. There is a story in the family that, when I was about 6, Mum was planning a Christmas present for Dad. She was going to knit him a jersey and was planning this quietly in her own thoughts when I chirped up, 'You should knit it in brown because Daddy doesn't like Fair Isle.' I actually do remember saying this and also remember basking in the glory as my incredulous mother related this story to any relative who would listen over the next few years!

Immediately after Mum's death my younger sister Elizabeth had a series of vivid lucid dreams in which she and a much younger version of Mum were sitting on a bench in a garden (gardening was a significant pleasure in Mum's life and she was very good at it).They talked about my sister's children, her job as a teacher and all the ordinary, everyday things that families talk about. Finally, in the dream, Mum would turn to Liz and say, 'Well, I must be going now because your Dad will be waiting' and she'd walk away and my sister would wake up.

I was very distressed when I heard about these dreams and I felt rather hurt that I was excluded from the comfort and love my mother was extending to my sister. It felt as if in some way I wasn't grieving enough to warrant a dream of my own. Some years later on holiday with my partner in France I was admitted overnight to hospital in Cavaillon. I had had all the symptoms of a heart attack. In the early hours, lying on a trolley waiting for a cardiac ultrasound I heard my mother's voice very clearly say, *'I'm here with you Jack, not come for you.'* Hearing her voice as I lay in hospital telling me very clearly that she was with me I understood that in appearing to my sister in dreams she was responding to Liz's deep need and that at my own hour of need when I was afraid and lonely (despite a loving partner who had been with me throughout the night), she was extending the same comfort and reassurance and showing me that the connection between the world of Spirit and our own world is strong. Also, by saying that she had not "Come for me" she let me know that at the moment of our bodily death, we are met and helped to make the transition.

Throughout my life I have accepted an afterlife as a strong probability. To my mind it makes no sense at all to think that a creation as complex and extraordinary as a human being can cease to exist at the point of physical death. For the emotions, feelings, ingenuity, creativity and splendour of human consciousness to cease to exist at the death of the body is the equivalent of walking a cosmic plank! We simply can't drop off the end into nothingness! My "encounter" with my mother, or with her consciousness, was a confirmation of this lifelong acceptance and I am truly grateful to have experienced it. My Mum was a very talented and extremely dedicated gardener and after her death there were days when I felt her close as I worked in my own garden.

Jackie Bartlett

I have been a Friend for forty years and a Spiritualist for 6 years. This year (2011) I had an experience which for me confirms the truth of spiritual survival. I had spent months doing a portrait of my late wife from a photograph, and finally reached a point beyond which I could not go! So, having cleaned all my equipment, I sat down in front of the canvas. After a few minutes I experienced a strong pull between my solar plexus and the painting. The same evening as I put my foot on the first step to go upstairs to bed I heard a voice at the back of my head behind the right ear, saying simply, 'Good night' ! I have never had such an experience before or since! I am 82 and hope to develop further, but who knows!

John Lawton

Since my husband, Martin, died from cancer in December 2003 I have visited Paul Lambillion, a gifted and experienced healer, channeller, and spiritual counsellor on several occasions. Paul had given Martin two sessions of spiritual healing. The second took place only two days before his death and I am sure it helped him to make the transition as quickly and smoothly as he did.

Martin was one of the founder members of QFAS and had been fully convinced of the reality of the after-life for many years. A month after his death I visited Paul, and Martin communicated. Though Paul does not call himself a medium, he is aware of beings on other levels and Martin "popped through" (as Paul describes it) to give convincing proof that he still continued to be very much himself and was aware of the doings of myself and his family on Earth. His individual sense of humour was particularly in evidence!

In later communications, as I grew more confident and started to ask questions, Martin explained about his transition and how he was now occupied.

Briefly, Martin explained that his first impression after he "died" was that he was in a kind of waiting room and was met by his father and another man who he described but who I could not identify. He then received some teaching from a spiritual being and was also given a map to show him where he had come from and what were the future possibilities. The map was very significant as Martin was a planner by profession and was always happy and relieved if given a map to find his way around! He explained that the newly arrived are received and given information in a form which feels most natural to them.

Martin said that as soon as he died, though he had resisted the idea of death while still on Earth, he realised that it was absolutely the right moment for him to go. He was being given the opportunity, he said, to create something beautiful, and it was right for him to "move through" to do this. We should not look at death as in any way the end, but as a stepping through to a new level, equipped with all our recent life experience.

His task now is to work with the spirits of the mineral kingdom in the changes which are taking place on the planet. (He described other things he is doing but this is his main work.) He finds his new work "enthralling", and he says there are big changes coming which will be beneficial in the long term, and that possibly new minerals may emerge from the "heat of the planet".

In his retirement Martin was a potter with a particular love of unusual glazes. As he worked with minerals to create these, his life-long interest in geology was finding a new outlet. He says now that all that he learned on Earth is combining to help him in his new task.

Perhaps we should not wonder too much when we feel the desire to add a new piece of knowledge or experience into our lives. It may build towards helping us in our after-life work.

Angela Howard

I have been granted – much to my surprise – two short, telepathic verbal exchanges with my wife who had died eighteen months before. Both occurred in the context of a Quaker Meeting for Worship, a service which is well-known to produce an atmosphere conducive to telepathy.

The first occurred following my birthday in February 2006. I was on my way to join the weekly mid-day Quaker Meeting in Oxford, while I was also searching for a couple of cut-glass tumblers that I needed at home. I saw a couple of whisky tumblers in Boswell's, sitting on a cut-glass tray. I thought they would do, but I had no time to spare at that moment.

A little later, sitting in the silent Meeting, I got the impression that Betty was sitting on my left, as she used to do. So I inclined my head and sent out the thought, 'Hullo dear - nice to know you're with us today'. I had done this regularly whenever I felt her presence. I never expected any response – but on this occasion, a few seconds later, my mind was filled with her 'silent voice' saying, 'I liked the glasses on their tray and I'd be happy if you would buy them as a birthday present from me'. At that moment it seemed quite natural that Betty should answer me in that way and I was delighted. I turned my head and replied, 'That's a lovely idea, darling. Thank you. Yes, I'll do that'. That was all. I bought them on the way back.

I often, at that period, felt her presence with me at Meeting on Sunday mornings, but on the Sunday some ten days after the above I failed to get this impression. So I sent out the thought, 'Are you there, darling? I can't tell whether you're there or not.' Immediately, without any break, my mind was filled with her indignant reply, 'Of course I'm here. I'm always with you. Where else should I be?' This hot reply left me speechless, not only by its vehemence but because she ought not to be 'always with me'. It sounded as though she had no idea that she should be somewhere else, getting on with her new life with her family and friends. It sounded as if she were "earthbound", which was not healthy. So, when I felt her presence next at home I told her that, nice as it was to have her with me, I was sure she ought to be elsewhere. I assured her I'd be alright here until the time when I would come over and be with her again...   In my next prayer session I asked my "Guardians" to exercise any influence they might have with Betty to get her moving in the right direction. I've not felt her presence at all since then.

There was one final act in the story. A few nights later, in another prayer session, my mind was filled with the following thought from Spirit, 'In the past you spent years ordering people about in your present life. Now you've started ordering them about in the next!' It's true that I occupied a managerial position for many years, but I never "ordered people about" in that sense. But I'm very glad to know that my "Guardians" have a lively sense of humour.

H. Dennis Compton

One day my daughter told me this story. Not long before, my son-in-law's uncle Frank had passed away. He was elderly and had had numerous things wrong with him for a very long time. My daughter, Dianne, and husband, Paul, had done a lot for him, shopping and helping him with difficult paperwork. After his wife died he used to come and have Christmas dinner with us all, but for the last two years he wasn't well enough. This year Dianne cooked it for him and delivered it to his house before the rest of us sat down to have ours.

Uncle Frank had made a will. He didn't have a lot of money to leave because he'd put his house into equity, but there would be some, and it was important it went to the right persons. Dianne and Paul would not inherit directly, but there was a slight possibility they might receive a small amount indirectly. Unfortunately, the will couldn't be found and if it didn't turn up soon the money would be distributed to the wrong people. Dianne and a relation of Uncle Frank's, Betty, had been making visits to the house to tidy up and see to a few things. They hunted high and low for the will, which was in the house somewhere, but it didn't turn up and the date for the allocation of the money was almost upon them. Dianne was so worried.

'Uncle Frank, Uncle Frank, you've got to help me find your will,' she said. 'You've got to help me.'

That night she dreamt of a biscuit box and she remembered it in the morning. She and Betty went back to the house that Saturday and combed it from top to bottom but no will or biscuit box appeared. They retired to the car greatly disheartened. 'I'm going back in,' said Dianne. 'I'm going to have one more look.'

At the side of the house was a walkway which Uncle Frank had covered over and converted into a utility room where he kept his washing machine and a few other things. Nothing much, and, as Dianne said afterwards, it simply wasn't the sort of place where you would leave a will. They had looked there before, of course, but maybe because it was such an unlikely place, they hadn't taken any notice of the biscuit box on the shelf. After all, you don't keep wills in biscuit boxes, do you? As soon as they saw it Dianne pounced. Inside were tins of shoe polish. She was so disappointed. The two of them decided that was it. They gave up. Dianne put the lid back on the tin and picked up some rubbish on the shelf below to throw in the bin. But first she took it into the sitting room to make sure there was nothing of importance there. It didn't look like it: a few pieces of scrap paper and a scruffy-looking blank brown envelope. She peered inside the envelope and … there was the will. Not in the biscuit box, but right underneath it on the shelf below.

Shirley Walford

Approximately 30 years ago, when I became interested in Spiritualism, I read about the books which Hugh Dowding had written during World War II. I came across *Lychgate* and *Many Mansions*, in a second-hand bookshop. Wishing to find out more about the man, my husband and I visited Moffat in the Scottish Borders just 60 miles away. There we visited the Museum. That is where I met Irene.

Hugh had spent his early years in Moffat where his father was headmaster of the Academy. The school motto was "Manners makyth man" - inscribed over the fireplace, which very much reflected Hugh's character. To cut a long story short, over many decades the school fell into disrepair and was in a bad state. Irene had been born in Moffat. During the war she was a meteorologist in the WAAF. She had never personally met Hugh. She knew of his Spiritualism and the work he had done on his retirement, giving talks to anxious families in London, and reassuring the souls who found themselves on the other side.

After the war Irene made it her business to renovate the Academy which had been his home. Hugh had died in the meantime. Irene's plan was to make it into accommodation for wounded RAF personnel. She completed her task.

She showed me around the building in Well Street, Moffat. It is beautifully appointed. A lace curtain depicts the Battle of Britain. A bronze bust of Sir Hugh Dowding stands in the capacious hallway. The school motto is in place inscribed over the fireplace. Irene herself was not a Spiritualist, although very sympathetic. Her fiancé had been killed in battle. However one day a medium contacted her to say that 'Sir Hugh Dowding wishes to thank her for all she has done'. Irene and I became good friends and remained in touch for many years. We often spoke about spiritual things.

Eileen Blenkinsop

I suppose I must have been about four years old when my mother started leaving me with Mrs Cain while she went on the bus to go shopping in Leeds. Mrs Cain was a dear old lady whom I grew to love very much. I called her my second mother. These were the war years, and she had a daughter of her own who worked in an aircraft factory. I never passed her cottage without calling in to see her and I sang carols at Christmas knowing she would give me a penny or two.

I went round to see Mrs Cain one day and found her daughter Edith in the kitchen. Edith said her mother was in bed because she wasn't very well. I could go up to see her, but if she was asleep I was not to wake her. I went upstairs but Mrs Cain was asleep. I was disappointed and came downstairs without waking her, as Edith had said.

Some days or weeks later, I caught measles or mumps or chicken pox or something, and had to stay in bed. One morning my mother came upstairs and said she was going to the pictures. It wasn't like my mother to leave me alone in the house and I knew the cinema wasn't open, but I said nothing and let the mystery pass me by.

When I was well enough to come downstairs my mother told me Mrs Cain had died and she had been to her funeral. That explained the mystery. I can't remember if I said or just thought, 'I didn't have a chance to say goodbye'.

Sometime later I seemed to know I was dreaming. I saw myself standing at the front doorway of my aunts' cottage and I saw Mrs Cain standing behind the garden gate. 'I've come to say goodbye,' she said. In my dream I saw myself turn into the house and call to my aunts, 'Mrs Cain isn't dead. She's here. Come and look'. I turned back to look outside, but Mrs Cain had gone. There was no-one else. I have never seen her since.

Anne Arundel

*Anne Arundel, mother of our CD secretary, **David**, was a very enthusiastic member of QFAS whom many will remember meeting at conferences. She died peacefully on 13th November, 2016, aged 77. David has sent this account of a contact he received in January 2018.*

I went to a spiritualist church two weeks ago for the first time in years and, although nothing happened then, when I went again last Wednesday the medium came to me with lots of messages from my mother. Her identity was verified first of all, then there were lots of detailed messages about things which showed my mother was up-to-date with what had been going on around me and my brother and the outer family.

Most of the messages I could take, but two I could not. One was asking me if I knew anyone who had been on holiday in a caravan at Filey, and the other was asking me did I know of anyone who had lost a dog?

The next day, however, I was in contact with my godmother who was with my mother in her final days, and told her everything that had happened. I discovered that one of my godmother's daughters had recently lost a dog, and her other daughter had been to Filey in a caravan, twice! Both my brother and I and my godmother and the outer family have been stunned by the information that came through. I am wondering whether my mother gave the two messages which meant nothing to me with the particular intention of convincing others.

David Arundel

On 24th February 2016, my oldest and very close friend, made the transition we know as death. She was just 71 and in good basic health, despite some ongoing health issues. Her death was virtually instantaneous as she fell to the floor, having a few seconds previously been laughing and chatting to someone, and having just cycled through a park on a lovely February morning. Her death was therefore totally unexpected and shocking to her family and to me, her friend since school, university, and for the 50 or more years after.

We had been continually in each other's lives, and she was a major reason why I had moved to Devon, to live near her so we could continue to share our lives. I hope I am not tempting providence in saying that I doubt whether I will ever sustain a greater shock. I continue to mourn her passing

The interesting thing was, that when I met my wife, I had an experience. I kissed her, and as I moved away, staring at me was my mother's face. And she said to me, 'Sixty-eight'. I knew straight away, without thinking, what she meant. My mother passed with cancer when she was sixty-eight.

My wife contracted cancer at sixty-eight and I lost her. I haven't lost her! She's still around me. I see her and I feel her. All the time. And my daughter sees her and talks to her. She's very mediumistic, too.

Another time, my friend, Janette, and I were driving over to Kent. We were driving down this lovely country lane on a summer's day and suddenly I was raised out of my body, while I was driving. I was lifted up, surrounded, embraced by love. And I knew it was my wife. At the end of the lane was a cross roads, and a village. I hadn't realised before that this was a place my wife and I had visited on our last day out before she died. She was very ill but we'd had a nice day out and sat by the sea in the sunshine. And she caught me up to remind me of where I was. I'd had no idea. We'd come there a different way. The experience took my breath away. It was mind blowing – especially as I was driving! And it showed me that the love that we share is never lost. It can do nothing but grow, and we can never separate.

John Philps

I feel very close to my Aunt Sylvia (Sylvy). She was only eight years older than me so felt more like my sister.

When her husband Phillip passed on, aged 92 years, we had a little sitting or perhaps it was more like a Quaker Meeting; simply three of us, Don my husband, Sylvy and myself staying in the silence together.

There was an empty chair to my left and I gradually became aware that Phillip was sitting there. Mentally I thanked him for coming but said that I needed something to prove he was really there and that I was not imagining his presence. He seemed glad to be with us and happy and well. I repeated my request and as I looked to my left I saw a catapult appear in a flash on the seat of the chair and then it disappeared.

After our quiet time Sylvy asked if we had felt, heard or seen anything as we turned inward. I said that I had felt Phillip's presence with us and his gentle personality but I laughed; all that I had seen was a quick flash of a catapult resting on the seat of the chair to my left.

Sylvy sat up quickly and asked if I had known that when my father died my mother had given his catapult to Phillip. I did not know and had completely forgotten that my father had one! He had a long garden with lots of vegetables and used to scare off visiting cats with warning shots nearby! This for me was clear proof that Phillip had been present. He showed me something I would never have guessed and did not know about.

I now have the catapult in a small drawer in the desk/bureau where I write letters in our front study. It brings back memories of several lovely people.

Mahalla Mason

I often think what a pity it is that for the greater part of my life I did not know what now I do know: that the 'dead' are around us, and can help us in ways we may not be conscious of. This truth, known to primitive peoples in many parts of the world, is being denied and ignored in our materialistic, science driven society.

In 1976 my husband Roy died very suddenly of coronary thrombosis, at the age of 53. It was a cruel blow - no warning, no opportunity to say the last things to each other - and my recovery was slow. Healing really started when I discovered Claridge House and became involved in the Friends (and much laughter!). Looking back I can see that I was guided there.

In the eighties there was an upsurge of accounts of near-death experiences. Having heard such an account first-hand from a Friend at a Woodbrooke Easter gathering, I felt assured that at least Roy was in a good place. I have always been convinced that life cannot end in death, but Roy himself had not been religious and viewed life after death as a remote possibility. He was very much living in the here and now, involved in his career, in the house we were doing up, and our life together.

In 1993 a friend told me about his visit to the College of Psychic Studies in London where a medium put him in touch with his wife, who had died not long before. She appeared very happy and delighted to let him know this. It encouraged me to follow his example and make an appointment, and what I hoped for happened: Roy made contact through the medium, a kind older woman with a lovely voice. From the start I had no doubt that it was Roy communicating through her - what he said about his reactions to what had happened to him was so very much in character.

He told me what a terrible shock his death had been to him. First of all he had to realise that he had died and that was hard, and then that he was alive in a different dimension. If only he had had some warning - he felt it was unfair to have been plucked out of life, and at first he was angry and bitter and he raged against it. But he was given much healing and rest and loving care. My mother spent a lot of time talking with him and that too helped him to come to terms.

He told me that without his body, and the feeling of status he had worked for in life, he felt he was a different being: in fact he felt a speck, a microcosm in the macrocosm. It cost him much effort to accept himself as a spiritual being; only slowly did he get the feeling that the spiritual self is more valuable than the physical self.

He spoke of the colours he was often wrapped around in – 'the colour is not just a colour, it is a vibration around you and through you, healing and revitalising you. It's wonderful you know, I have not got over the wonder of it yet.' Roy also told me that our two cats, who had died a few years earlier, were with him, and that my present cat could see him when he was in the house.

He wanted me to know that he was always around in the evening when I got ready for bed, and that he wrapped me around with his love as I went to sleep. He felt closer to me now than had been possible in life. This session with Roy took away any doubts I had about the veracity of this kind of communication. It was so totally true, and it changed my life to know that Roy is around me often, and that we shall meet again in the next life - because love cannot die.

Later, I was given some further assurances of Roy's presence in our house. One summer evening I had to go out and when I came home it was still light. Walking into the sitting room I was surprised to see a book in the middle of the carpet, closed, standing upright on its long side. As the house had been locked while I was out, there was no way this could have been done by human hand. I felt sure this had to be a signal from Roy - he loved making me laugh, and I did laugh when I saw it was my house-plant book. I had not been too successful with some of my plants and was obviously being told I needed to consult the book a bit more!

On a later occasion I saw something very small in a dark corner of the room which certainly had not been there that morning when I hoovered the carpet. It was a pretty cowrie shell with an unusual pattern in violet and brown. Later it was followed, at intervals, by two other small delicate shells which arrived in times of stress, giving me once again the reassurance that I am not alone in the house. Of course I treasure these little love tokens.

I have written this because Roy has urged me to. He wanted it known that without any preparation the transition into the next life can be difficult - but that there is help, and all shall be well.

Joanna Harris

Six years ago, when I was sitting beside my husband who was drifting in and out of consciousness – he talked to unseen friends. I had a feeling they were standing around his bed waiting for him. I knew, by the names he used, that they had been in the Army together in 1939 and had been killed. He told them about how he was wounded and had met me – it appeared to be a complete conversation. Some months after his death I experienced a black day – it was then I heard his voice saying, 'Let me go'.

My daughter, Ruth, is a reflexologist and had a new client visit her. As he walked through the door he stopped and said, 'There are three men standing behind you and one is saying you were right.' He gave brief descriptions and said, 'The last one says his name is Bobby.' She then told him that one was her brother who died last year, aged 46, and had not believed in the afterlife. The second was my husband and her father, and the third her Grandad, who was always known to the children as Grandad Scotland. His name was Robert by the way! When she related all this to me we had to decide whether to tell my daughter-in-law (who had suffered severe depression since last year). When the time was right I just told her of the visit and asked if she would like to hear about it. A few months later she asked Ruth to tell her.

Mary Farquhar

Books can speak to us in many ways. They can inform us, thrill us, inspire us and enlighten us. My own experiences suggest that they may also be used as instruments of psychical communication, bridging the gap between this world and the next and demonstrating the survival of the human personality after death? My book, *A Study in Survival: Conan Doyle Solves the Final Problem*, (O Books), describes how I was forced slowly, and at times reluctantly, to accept that I was able to communicate by a most remarkable method with a most remarkable man, who had died eleven years before I was born. That man was the creator of Sherlock Holmes, Sir Arthur Conan Doyle, who had devoted the last fourteen years of his life to publicising the evidence for life after death to a world-wide audience.

The simple method of communication which developed involved Conan Doyle's own writings, of which I have a large collection. *A Study in Survival* describes how the whole extraordinary saga began, completely unexpectedly, with what Sherlock Holmes would have called "the curious incident of the dog in the night-time", when a much loved dog of mine died one evening at my home.

To take my mind off worries that he might have suffered at the end, I casually opened the first book lying on my bedside table. This happened to be a thick volume of collected (non-Sherlockian) short stories by Conan Doyle, and with my thoughts elsewhere, still firmly fixed on the dog, I opened it completely at random and glanced at the page. The first words my eyes fell upon were: *"his exit was as speedy and painless as could be desired."* To my amazement I found that the reference was to the death of a dog – *"the poor little doggie."* In something of a daze, I turned back to the page before, and at once a sentence seemed to stand out as if highlighted. It read: *"A more malignant case I have never seen."* What was this case? The answer appeared a couple of lines earlier– the case in question was *"a frightful sarcoma."* I almost fell out of bed! My vet had recently diagnosed that my dog was suffering from a malignant sarcoma, a term which I was then unfamiliar with.

Was all this an amazing coincidence? To test this, I began experimenting with a more deliberate and "interactive" approach. Instead of just opening a book at random, I would sometimes deliberately formulate a particular question or concern, either in my mind or out loud, and then close my eyes to make a completely blind selection from the long shelf of Conan Doyle volumes that I possessed. Without looking at the title, I would then open the book completely at random and focus on the first words my eyes fell upon. I would not know in advance which book from a shelf six feet long would be used and this would often turn out to be an obscure volume which I had not read for years. This method produced and continues to produce remarkable results, and I now have records of many hundreds of such "readings". These cover an extensive range of topics and subjects in which Conan Doyle might reasonably be expected to have a special interest or particular expertise. They include medical matters, sporting events, military and political affairs, cryptic puzzles and religious topics. Conan Doyle's sense of humour is often evident and the sense of interacting with a powerful personality is very strong.

The results have gone far beyond what could be expected by way of chance, often involving amazingly specific detail relevant to the issue in question. Many of these are fully described in *A Study in Survival*, and I will give only one brief example here. Current news items have proved to be a rich source of material, which was consistent with Conan Doyle's intense interest in current affairs. So, stunned like everyone else by the 9/11 attack on the World Trade Centre in New York, I that evening asked for a comment. On blindly selecting a book, my eyes fastened at once on six words in the middle of the top line of the page: *"In New York, in the centre."*

My experiences also resulted in a memorable correspondence with Conan Doyle's daughter, Jean, shortly before her death. By means of random readings from her father's books, I was able quite unknowingly to give her the correct answer to a test question of hers, designed to confirm her father's identity. 'No living soul would have known that information,' she told me.

Roger Straughan

(*A Study in Survival: Conan Doyle Solves the Final Problem*, by Roger Straughan, is published by O Books, Ropley, UK, www.o-books.net, ISBN: 978 1 84694 240 2)

(I had been emailing Roger about the piece above, and when I switched off the computer I idly turned on the TV. The first words to come from it were, "It's Arthur Conan Doyle." When the picture and words had settled

I realised I had switched on in the middle of a quiz programme and had obviously heard the answer to a question. It seemed an extraordinary coincidence, but completely in keeping with Roger's own experience.
Angela Howard.)

Take time to learn about other people's experiences of the Light. Remember the importance of the Bible, the writings of Friends and all writings which reveal the ways of God. As you learn from others can you in turn give freely from what you have gained? While respecting the experiences and opinions of others, do not be afraid to say what you have found and what you value. Appreciate that doubt and questioning can also lead to spiritual growth and to a greater awareness of the Light that is in us all.

Advices and queries: 5

3.22

Now there are varieties of gifts, but the same Spirit; and there are varieties of services, but the same Lord; and there are varieties of activities, but it is the same God who activates all of them in everyone. To each is given the manifestation of the Spirit for the common good. (1 Cor 12: 4-7)

It is a responsibility of a Christian community to enable its members to discover what their gifts are and to develop and exercise them to the glory of God.

(Quaker Faith & Practice, 1995.)

3. NEAR DEATH EXPERIENCES

The Near Death Experience (NDE) is a phenomenon which has gained increasing recognition in our times. This is partly the result of improved resuscitation techniques enabling those close to death to be brought back from the brink to recount their experience.

Raymond Moody's book Life After Life *(pub.1975) caused a breakthrough which enabled many people to feel that for the first time it was safe to recount experiences they had been afraid to speak about for fear of ridicule.*

It is important to note that not all NDEs are as positive as the ones recounted in this section. There are the so-called negative NDEs which could perhaps be the result of a life of crime and violence and might have value in pointing the way towards the need for change.

A Friend related to me a true and very thought-provoking story.

It concerned a lady she knew who, whenever she hears an ambulance siren, sends up a mental prayer, or thought, for the person involved in the incident. She thinks something such as, 'If this person is not going to recover then please let their passing be pain-free, gentle and peaceful – and, if they *are* going to recover then let their recovery be full and complete, and may they have no debilitating after effects.'

One day she was passing the scene of a road accident, and she sent up her usual prayer. Sometime later, she was at some sort of gathering, and a lady came up to her and said, 'Oh, I've been looking for you. I'm so glad I've found you!'

'I'm sorry, but I don't know you. I don't think we've ever met,' said the other, rather mystified. 'Well', said the stranger, 'not long ago I had a road accident, and during the time the paramedics were treating me, I almost died. I passed out of my body and looked down on the scene. And I saw you there, and received the thoughts you sent up for me. I have been waiting to thank you!'

Rosalind Smith

Having been a member of the Friends Fellowship of Healing for many years, upholding others in the Divine Light, and having myself been embraced by the loving thoughts and prayers of others (many unknown to me) when I have been very ill, has been a positive experience. We are all wounded healers.

I wrote an article for the FFH Journal, *Towards Wholeness,* on 'Out of Body Experiences', two of which I had in hospital in 2003 as a result of anaphylactic shock due to multiple drug and food allergies (all brought about as a result of being on statins and aspirin 75mg for a short time). On several occasions my husband had been warned I might not recover.

On every occasion there has been an OBE (out of body experience), I have never had a sense of going through a dark tunnel, but have immediately found myself to be in a place of great Light.

Friends I have known, loved and supported whilst they were on earth and whom I had walked with during their final illnesses and been privileged to be present at their passing over from this life to the next, I found them all there in welcome. They were all bathed in glorious Light, looking young, about 25 –30, and their real spiritual presence was totally recognisable. Beyond them was such a radiant Light, words cannot express it. I felt totally unworthy and unable to look into this Light which surrounded me, but experienced such strong feelings of love and acceptance coming towards me.

There was not a full Life Review, only brief glimpses of certain events that had occurred on Earth. I felt sorrow for misdeeds and for hurting friends and family, and full of gratitude for having had a good home, family life and friends.

I most definitely did not want to return to Earth and occupy my Earthly body. (I am quite disabled due to multiple sclerosis, osteoporosis, and have severe swallowing problems, living mostly on artificial nutrition as I refuse to have a naso-gastric tube or a PEG fitted.)

The sense of joy, expanded consciousness, a feeling of wholeness, awareness of realities one could only glimpse and wanting to learn more, was quite overwhelming.

The last OBE was when I was being resuscitated in Casualty one Sunday morning in 2013 just before Quaker Meeting for Worship was about to start. Michael, my husband, phoned a dear friend and Elder in our Meeting, to say I was very ill. The Friend asked Meeting to uphold Michael and myself in the Divine Light. All I knew was that I was high up in a beautiful cloudy sky, surrounded by radiant Light, looking down on the hospital. I was drawn to the body on the bed in "Resuss", where there was an Indian Doctor on one side and a Senior Staff Nurse on the other. Seeing the way they were taking such care of this 'fitting' body filled me with compassion and gratitude. It took some time before I realised the body was mine, the one I inhabited whilst on Earth. Not wanting to leave my husband alone (we have now been married 44 years), and sensing my time had not yet come, I 'jumped back' into my body. How angry I was with the Doctor and Nurse when I regained consciousness and felt so ill again! I did apologise later.

This sense of what some people might describe as 'being nearly dead' left me with a strong impression that who I was on Earth, what my social standing was, who I was related to, was totally unimportant. There was a wonderful sense of knowing that I was a complete spiritual being who was part of something greater.

Plato saw the soul liberated at last from the body in which it had been imprisoned, and returning to the realm of pure ideas. This links up with the words of T.S. Eliot, when he writes of the full circle of life:-

In my beginning is my end –
... In my end is my beginning.

Those of us living with life-threatening conditions see life going on all around us: people going about their normal business as though they would live forever, whereas 'normal' for us is often feeling physically and mentally more and more tired and living in a parallel universe. At such times, especially after diagnosis, it is as if we walk into a glass wall and realise that nothing is the same anymore. Our bodies can become quite strange and alien to us, as though they are not really ours. We can help others so struggling to remember that they are still whole and unique individuals. I often say, "I am not my body."

Pat Pilkington, co-founder of the BCHC (Bristol Cancer Help Centre) uses the "Hero's journey of myth", as an archetype or metaphor for the cancer experience: - "The Hero leaves all that is familiar, comfortable and companionable, and in the dark before dawn, rises alone and sets off to journey to the far country. It takes consummate courage and faith to face the 'Dragon Fear' and rescue the 'Maiden': the true Self. The Hero returns, changed by the experience."

What do I feel I have learned from the OBE episodes? I am not afraid of death although naturally concerned about what I may have to go through during the dying process. In particular there is a fear of becoming totally dependent on others, a burden to those I love, and loss of dignity. A common fear of many.

At times when I am really ill I am envious of others who have already returned to whence they came. Generally I am more aware telepathically of events to come, precognition, intuition, not dreams. It is usually when I am doing something quite mundane like washing dishes when I just "know" something good is happening, someone is dying or someone urgently needs to be upheld in prayer, and I quite often know who it is even if previously all has been well with them.

There is a greater awareness than before of "seeing" another's pain, anguish, hidden trauma or anxieties. Sometimes I "see a new soul preparing to come to Earth", a baby boy or girl, before the parents are aware of it. This happened when I saw a baby boy in the foetal position head down ready for birth above the head of our Quaker Elder Friend's wife, three months before she was pregnant.

I have been aware of souls exiting the body at time of transition, and also, before the parents have realised this, when a soul has left its developing embryo. The last example was four Christmases ago when two young friends excitedly told me they were going to have another baby. This was when the mother to be was about nine weeks pregnant and they were not yet generally sharing the news. As they told me this after Quaker Meeting, I "sensed" that the soul of a baby boy had already left its body. Shortly after the mother miscarried a son.

I believe that death is the next step in our pilgrimage, the gateway, the opening of the welcoming adventure of the next step we take when we leave our human bodies and enter the realm of pure spirit from whence we came.

This is a lesson we must all learn – letting go and being willing to let go, but also to continue the journey. We must not cling to life or seek to die, but live each day, each moment, knowing that as long as we continue the pilgrimage, we have something to give and something to gain.

How do we know? We do not know with our minds, but we believe in the depths of our hearts as we have complete trust and faith in the Holy Spirit, Divine Light, Source of all Creation, whatever you believe in which has enlightened your way. I believe so strongly that the soul of man or woman never sleeps and is never unconscious, however we may appear to others. Reincarnation too also helps to makes sense of what we undergo in this life as we walk or travel through Keats' 'vale of soul-making': our spiritual journey on Earth.

We can only pray, God give us strength, strength to hold on and strength to let go.

Isobel Bracewell

Taken from a sermon given at a church in Norfolk on 31st December 2017. The author is an Anglican priest as well as a Quaker.

Now a New Year approaches, an adventure is ahead for all of us as it was for Jesus' parents. How I approach the New Year is affected by an experience I dare to share with you. It was an experience that made me ask: how can I discern what God is saying to me and how is he calling me to use my time on this earth?

Following an operation at St Luke's hospital in London, I suffered a septic shock. As I recovered from it I heard the nurse saying she could not find a pulse, and later she told me this had been for about 30 seconds. During that time I had a clear sense of figures standing before me, backlit by a powerful light, and just as I prepared to join them I became aware of an oxygen mask clamped to my face, and of nurses and a doctor in my room.

As I thought about the experience, I realise I had a glimpse of what I understand as the world to come, the kingdom of heaven, but the description that seems to fit most closely is 'the world of light'. It seemed the strongest light was some distance away from me, not exactly along a tunnel as others have described, but just some way off, and that the figures that came towards me had a distinct quality. The understanding I have now, and one affirmed by others who have had contact with such an experience, is that in the world of light our senses are more fully available to us. It is not that they are limited by our physical humanity but rather that they expand infinitely, giving the ability to fully sense and grasp things that we see only partly in this present life, as St Paul described it. The figures I saw seemed also to be able to move freely, and I feel this points to a world where there are more than three dimensions. There remains something which enables recognition, but there are also extra dimensions which allow different kinds of movement and appearance to those which are human.

The Jamaican consultant came soon after and said, 'You were not ready to go to your Maker', and I responded: 'There is lots more I want to do with my life'. I had to think more fundamentally about what God requires of me during the remaining years he has given me. I found a helpful piece of advice by Jenifer Faulkner in the *Quaker Faith and Practice*: "The real tragedy is not how or when we die but if we do not live the life we are given to our full potential."

We can all make the coming New Year one of the most significant times of our lives. We need to make the most of our living. We need not so much to make resolutions as to make the most of all our opportunities.

Service to one another can be part of deciding how we live. We can recognise that there is that of God in each person he has made. Let us concentrate on people, show them that we care, and hold them in love and compassion.

Peter Varney

Amongst several mystical experiences described by Len (the late father of a friend) was one describing a minor operation that he had to remove the pus from a whitlow on his finger in about 1950. He had noticed that the patient before him had struggled while the anaesthetic mask was placed over his nose, occasioning the doctor to say 'Keep still!' Good God man, we're not trying to kill you!', so Len determined that when it came to his turn he would take a particularly deep breath of anaesthetic.

As soon as he did so he found himself floating above the operating table, at about 8 or 9 feet. He looked down and saw his own body on the table and the doctor making the incision. He wasn't bothered by this but continued to float upwards until he was very high and entered into a hall with golden fluted pillars. Near the top there was an eagle's claw and held in the claw was a crimson ball of about four or five feet in diameter.

He was then flipped onto his feet and was standing in beautiful country with sunshine and blue sky and there was a privet hedge about six feet high that was glittering as if with diamonds, which may have been dew drops in the sunshine. He followed the hedge and saw a cottage and a lovely garden with flowers of all colours and types. Then he saw a lady dressed in old fashioned clothes and with a hair style of the same period. He seemed to recognise her and felt that he had come home and had 'a wonderful feeling of bliss'. She smiled at him as though she knew him and he went to her because he wanted to embrace her, but then she moved as though she was afraid. At that point he heard a voice in his head saying, 'Go back'. Straight away he woke up.

The doctors then asked him if he had had some kind of dream and he said, yes, it was a lovely dream and described what he had seen. The doctors said that he couldn't have seen the operation as he was 'totally out', but he was able to pinpoint where on his finger the incision had been.

He normally forgot dreams but he has never forgotten this experience which has always been as clear as he described it. At the time of the operation he had never heard of Out of Body or Near Death Experiences.

A QFAS member

This is part of a summary of a talk given by Vivian Barty Taylor to the QFAS conference held at Woodbrooke in 2017. At the age of ten years old Vivian was diagnosed with an inoperable brain tumour.

Before the birth of his first daughter, Vivian was facing a major operation. At the time he could have said that he had had a good life and was prepared to let go. Once he had children things were different because of the great parental love he feels. The operation was to remove eight drains from his head – pieces of plastic tubing, or shunts, which take fluid down into the abdomen. The first had been placed in his brain soon after his diagnosis at the age of ten. This was an extremely delicate operation as the brain was by now adhering to the tubing. It could have gone terribly wrong.

He was lying in his hospital bed the night before the operation and he was terrified. He went to sleep and woke at about three in the morning in a state of complete terror. He was shaking, unable even to cry. He found the will to pray to whatever energy there was around him. 'I asked for help to get through whatever was to come.'

He had a most extraordinary experience because he felt a warm, yellow energy pouring into his body. It dissolved the fear. The fear lessened progressively until it was gone.

Vivian Said: 'Since that night, I've not been scared of death. I lost my fear of death that night, aged 27. I've got a lot of life to live, I hope. And I've got the energy to live it. But when I die I know I'll go back to that light. It's waiting for me, and I'm not scared.

'I feel very privileged to have had that experience. Hardship makes us grow. My hardship helped me grow to that point and further. I want to say to you that there's nothing to be scared of. We're going to go back to that warm place, and it's absolutely fine. This physical structure will disintegrate but we're all right.

'I've always had a strong belief in the afterlife. As a child I saw spirits. I saw my grandfather when I was four. He'd been dead twenty years and he was walking up the stairs in the house where he'd died. A lot of children see these things. They're closer to the start of their lives and have much less rational processing going on. This changes in the teenage years.

'I saw other spirits as well. A couple of years after the diagnosis of my tumour I became aware that I could feel the presence of spirits, could feel energies around me. This progressed to the point where I could access the spiritual, or third, eye. Buddhists achieve this through years of meditation, progressing up through the chakras. They progress gradually towards this end. With me it was different. It was egotistical. I had a problem in the centre of my brain, near the pineal gland, and I had to force my consciousness into the centre of the brain to try and deal with it.'

Vivian Barty-Taylor

'I'm not so far away',
is what she sometimes seems to say.
Or is it my imagination,
my need to feel at peace,
to trust that all is well?

'There's nowhere else' -
unbidden come more words -
'I'm here, behind the scenes,
closer than touch,
in realms where time and space
exist no more.'

Then in the silence,
in the chill,
I listen for more help.
How forge those wings
to cross that gulf
and take me where she is?

'Stay where you are'
her voice calls out.
'Your tasks are in the here and now,
and if you do them well
those wings will grow
and you will fly,
but not to somewhere else;
just closer still
to what is real,
to those you love so much.'

Jonathan Stedall

4. ANIMALS AND THE AFTERLIFE

For many people the death of a much loved companion animal can be almost as devastating as the loss of a human being. There is ample evidence that animals who have formed bonds with humans do continue into an afterlife and will be there to greet us when we too pass over. Cats and dogs, in particular, can be seen, heard or felt as spirit beings after their passing and in addition have their own awareness of the spirit world whilst on Earth.

I found a starving and bedraggled cat on my compost heap. I recognised her as Sukie who was left behind when my neighbours moved away. I took her into the warm and gave her some food and water. When I went to bed, she was curled up asleep at the end of it. In the night, I was woken by her crying whilst having 3 very premature kittens on my bed! Only one was living, looking like a stick insect, as he had no fur.

Sukie appeared to be very weak and sick and had no milk to give the kitten, who was trying to feed. As it was 2 am, I rang the emergency vet. She asked me to bring mother and baby to the surgery in my car. She stabilised Sukie and gave her an injection to bring in her milk. Meanwhile, she showed me how to feed the kitten with a pipette. But she said it would be a miracle if he lived through the night as he was much too premature.

I took them both home and settled them on a blanket in a cardboard box. Then went back to bed myself. Before sleeping, I held them both in the Light (i.e. Quaker healing). In the morning, Sukie already had milk and was suckling the tiny kitten who I now named Miracle! For the next 24 years, Sukie and Miracle lived happily together and were inseparable. They were very good companions to me. One day, Sukie became very sleepy and didn't want her dinner. She died a few hours later with Miracle curled up beside her. I laid her body in a box and lit a candle so Miracle and I could say goodbye. Then I took her body to the vet to be cremated.

Miracle lived 2 more years, but often seemed to be sad and missing his mother. Then he fell off the roof and had a dislocated hip, and broken leg. I took him to the vet and we decided he needed to be euthanised as he was in pain. I explained to him that he could go to join Sukie in Heaven, and asked his permission. The vet let me cuddle him whilst giving him the injection. But just before dying, Miracle looked up to the ceiling in a corner of the room. He gave the special mew with which he always greeted his mother. Evidently her spirit had come to escort him to the Afterlife. Then he stopped breathing.

Elizabeth M Angas

My husband John had a much loved dog called Lucy. About a year after she had died we were walking in a place where she had never been. We were not thinking or talking about her, when suddenly I saw her so clearly, her ears were up, eyes bright and shining and she was romping along enjoying the walk with us. It was a delightful thing to see and I was smiling. John turned to me and shaking his head said, 'I thought that I saw Lucy then'. I asked him where he thought that he had seen her. He pointed to the exact same place where she had been.

Robin Goodman

Two instances from friends come to mind, both concerning animals. The first from a friend who had recently had her cat put to sleep because of illness. She was distraught. Then in the garden her cat, Mimi, appeared, and led her through her old familiar haunts. She was happy. She looked back at her mistress and disappeared through the hedge.

Another friend was strongly aware, the night after her cat died, of purring and even the touch of whiskers from her cat on the bed. This latter friend is a very matter of fact person, not given to imaginings, and so positive about the experience.

Finally, an experience I had when walking next door's dog along the river bank. I was feeling rather down and was looking at the riverside plants. Suddenly and quite unexpectedly the greenery deepened in colour and I felt *so* surrounded with warmth and light – a very intense feeling. Again I had not expected this but know it happened.

Gill Sephton

My father, who was a well-known healer in Cornwall, was driving home one evening when he saw a cat lying motionless on the grass verge. It had evidently been hit by a car but was still conscious though severely injured. He stopped, picked it up, and took it to the nearest vet. Unfortunately the vet could not save it but said it must be euthanised. The following week my father had a reading with a medium. To his surprise, as he came into the room she told him, "There is a black cat walking beside you." He had never had a pet cat and supposed it must be the one he had taken to the vet a few days before. Perhaps a bond can be formed even in a short time when a last kindness is experienced this side of life.

Beryl Spence

My neighbour's cat went missing for a week in the August heatwave, and eventually was found under a bush in her garden, where it seemed he had returned to die, possibly of heatstroke. My friend, Thelma, aged 89, who has been a psychic medium for about 50 years, rang me in October and asked if I knew anyone whose cat had gone missing, describing a white cat with brown markings (exactly so), as he had just walked across her lounge! Thelma has rather a reputation for receiving visits from deceased animals

In 1978 I was a Senior Lecturer in History in the University of Hong Kong, living with my husband, an ethnic Russian from Latvia by origin. There was talk of paranormal events amongst people we knew. I forget the details now, but I remember being very curious about the whole question, and making something like a prayer, that before I left this world I might have some experience of these things. I thought no more of it, but some months later I took two clean pillowcases with other bed linen from a walk-in cupboard in our bedroom, to put clean linen on the bed. The pillowcases were the same colour. When I came to pick them up, there was only one. I was certain I took two, and searched the room and the cupboard. Then I called my husband, and he searched too. The thing had gone. There was nobody in the flat but us at the time, and I am certain I was alone in the room when the pillowcase disappeared.

A few months later I walked into the cupboard in our bedroom and there was the pillowcase, prominent on the shelf. It had not been there before. There now were two, as originally. My husband was not too surprised about this incident as he had told me that amongst the Russians such things often happen, and there is a belief that there is a house spirit called the Grandfather of the House (dedushka domovoi) who takes things for a while and brings them back.

In 1981 my husband died suddenly; a tremendous loss. Over the next few years there were occasions when he seemed to be speaking into my mind, but I could not be sure that my mind was not playing tricks.

In 1984 I retired, being by then Reader in History and nearly 61. When I got back to England and the flat we owned there, things began to happen in the mode of the pillowcase. The first event was so dramatic and extraordinary that I hesitate to tell it, because it sounds just like a story. But I am convinced that my husband brought me something that I needed, a thing of little material value but very useful to me. I am sure it was him because I had been thinking "Oh, if only you were here you could soon fix this up". But it was totally unexpected. All the incidents were unexpected.

After that he did not bring me anything for years, but things disappeared and re-appeared after a kind of pattern, as if he was doing it to keep in touch, or announce his arrival after an absence. This went on till 1990, when I became close to my present, second husband. The incidents became more and more frequent, daily that is, and sometimes several times a day. I became convinced that my first husband did not want me to marry the second one. To give just one example: I went to evensong at the local church - at that time I used to attend there as well as Quaker meeting. I had two front door keys on rings with other keys, and suddenly one lot vanished. I didn't worry, as I had the other set, and I was sure my husband would bring the missing one back. I locked up and went to church. Needing to wipe my nose, I put my hand in my coat pocket. It was rather a small pocket, and had a tissue in it. I wiped my nose and put the tissue back, and the keys were in the pocket, where there had only been a tissue before. It was the right-hand pocket and the left one was empty as before. I am right-handed. There was the other set of keys in my bag where I had put them after I locked the front door.

Gradually my first husband seemed to become resigned and the events became rarer. On the day of my wedding to my new husband I seemed to feel a sense of peace and benediction. But it seems my first husband still "comes by" every few months at least, and I miss something for some time and it suddenly turns up in a place where it could not possibly have got to or fail to have been seen. Sometimes he has brought me things, but the things involved in all the incidents never have value in terms of this world. There was one exception but that was not of any great value. Once I did see something vanish, but I've never seen anything actually re-appear.

I told my first cousin, and closest living relative apart from my daughters, about it, and she told me when she had a similar experience. But she was very annoyed about it, and said she hoped "they" would never do it again. So far as I know "they" haven't.

Rosemary Carthew

Since losing my husband and soulmate, Bryan, in September, 2010, many unexplained incidents have occurred in my home and also in the lives of some of our friends. Examples are electrical malfunctions which are automatically corrected; e-mails and texts from unknown senders with appropriate information for me; "answers" to personal questions via relevant words on the radio or in newspapers; household items moved, to be found elsewhere, etc.

But the strangest of all these incidents is that of the moveable bedsocks! Dozens of times in the last seven years I have awoken in the night or early morning to find my bedsocks 'removed' and lying on the adjoining pillow, sometimes as if thrown there, other times laid neatly one on top of the other as if brand new. I usually sleep reasonably well, which I believe must be with his help in some way, and am constantly surprised by this mystery, which happens still (a new innovation recently is that just *one* bedsock came off!). Bryan was an ingenious "problem-solver" of a person, who I think would have made an easy transition and would want to reassure me of his continuing presence and love. And he has certainly found a novel way of doing it!

Jill Woods

Since the early 1980s I have had a series of experiences which have led me to an understanding that the human spirit lives on after this life in another dimension.

The experience that was seminal in bringing me to a belief in an afterlife also awoke in me a strong urge to find a spiritual path (or rather to re-discover my lost path) and led me after a few years to membership of the Society of Friends. It was at the time of my mother's terminal illness in 1981. Having suffered from Alzheimer's for ten years, my mother had faded away, physically and mentally, to a distressing state. She had not recognised me or my father for years. She was being nursed in the local hospital. She had bed sores and was being given large doses of morphine as pain control.

Her death had been expected for four days but her heart was strong and she lingered on. My father and I visited every day. We were grieving, but didn't expect or want, for her sake, any recovery.

During the night after the fourth day of this crisis situation, I woke suddenly at about 3 am, unusually for me as I was normally a sound sleeper. As I lay in bed, I was aware of feeling a mental turbulence and great distress that was wordless. There was a sense of psychic pain that I had never experienced before. It went on and on, in writhing images shot across with distress and terror. I was of course thinking of my mother and assumed that this experience was a result of the stress I'd been through during the last few days. Gradually, however, possibly because of an intuitive sense of what would alleviate the pain, I found myself thinking about incidents in my mother's childhood and and early life when I knew she had been very happy. As I did this, the painful images subsided. My mother's married life had been difficult and unfulfilling, but she had always talked with wistfulness about her contented childhood in rural Shropshire with her two sisters and her beloved mother. Now I seemed to be seeing scenes from that time passing in front of me, suffused in a radiant light and always with a feeling of the love that had surrounded her, and a sense of my grandma's goodness and caring.

Then finally those scenes faded away and I had a feeling of a wonderful light and overwhelming love and peace, and then a strong, almost physical, sense of my mother's soul being lifted upwards to where grandma awaited her. My thought was, 'She's at peace at last.' And then I went to sleep.

In the early morning there was a phone call from the hospital to tell us that my mother had died at 4 am. I realised that during my night-time wakefulness I'd been linked in with my mother in some way which I did not understand. It was a totally new experience for me, as I was in no way 'psychic', but my mother and I had always had a closeness that was sometimes telepathic. Later, when I described the experience to friends who were open to such possibilities, one or two explained it to me as my mother having made contact with me on a spiritual level as the time of her death approached, so that I could give her my help at the time she moved on.

Interestingly, since that first occasion, I have found that 'by chance' I've fairly often been around when people I know are close to death and, while not conscious of helping them in any way except through prayer, I have usually been the last person to see them. In the case of relatives living at a distance, they have on several occasions died soon after my visit, when before that they were lingering on.

I have come to see, through the experience of helping my mother's transition that I perhaps have, at a deep level but one which dying people may be aware of, an acceptance of death and a lack of fear, which reassures the person approaching death and allows them to let go of life. I consider this to be a grace which I'm sure the souls of my mother and grandma have helped gift to me, for which I am very grateful. I feel it to be a very blessed kind of healing.

The only friend in whom I felt able to confide about what happened at the time of my mother's death was a person who has also had three similar experiences of being present at someone's death, although I did not know this until I spoke to her of these things. The people involved were not ones with whom she was especially close at other times. One was a neighbour, one the uncle of her ex-husband and the third was an acquaintance. With one of them she felt herself to be helping them to hold on to life; it was an almost physical sense of pulling them back from the brink of death, and the person concerned did recover from a life-threatening illness. The other two people died, and she felt she was there with them to help them towards the light, and was able to do so, although it was hard for her.

My friend was very unhappy about these experiences which she found frightening and seeming to present her with too much responsibility. At the time that they occurred she was not strong physically or emotionally and these unwanted events intruded on her fragility. I do think, however, that discovering I had been through a similar incident made her feel less isolated and odd. I was cheered to hear about her experiences and it helped make sense of my own.

Jean Mathias

I'd like to share this story of an Indian lady known to me. I'll call her Rani (not her real name). Rani was very unhappy in her marriage. Her husband's cruelty extended to sending their son to another part of India to be brought up in a boarding school – which, it later transpired, was a 'school' in name only – and Rani was not permitted to visit her son. One day Rani resolved to leave her husband and start a new life. This was an extreme solution for a woman trapped in a traditional Indian marriage. What made it even more difficult and dangerous was Rani's decision to take her son with her. Rani's plan was to travel to the school and request a meeting with him. She hoped that this might present an opportunity for her to take her son away. Rani was well aware that although she was the boy's mother, as a woman she had no authority even to request a meeting.

As Rani expected, when she met with the school principal, he brushed aside her pleadings brusquely. As Rani was being dismissed the principal suddenly and unexpectedly seemed to have a change of heart, and permitted her to take her son out of school for two hours. When Rani's son was brought to her, she saw that he was underweight from being ill-fed, was poorly dressed in thin clothes and had no shoes.

Once outside the school, the pair ran along roads and tracks to the nearest town. They joined the queue for a bus to Rani's chosen destination, a 'safe house' belonging to a distant relative. Rani had very little money, but she planned to travel by bus as far as the money would take them, then to complete the journey on foot. As they waited in the bus queue, Rani was extremely anxious in case her ploy had already been discovered. Then a woman appeared by Rani's side, and said, 'At a time like this, you need money', and the woman pressed something into Rani's hands. She glanced down in astonishment to see money in her hands. When she looked up again, the woman had vanished. Rani looked all around but the woman was not in the bus queue nor anywhere nearby. She had simply disappeared. Examining the money again, Rani saw that the cash was not just sufficient for the bus, but was a very large sum of money.

Rani did not stay long at the safe house. She knew that her husband would be very angry and would come looking for her. Rani feared for her life. As she was educated and had qualifications, she was able to obtain a visa entitling her to live and work in Britain. The money she had been given was enough to pay for her visa and flight to England and other necessary expenses. She made arrangements for her son to be well looked after in her temporary absence.

It was several years before it was reported back to Rani that her husband had given up looking for her, and it was safe to return to India. In the meantime, Rani had been able to save a lot more money towards the future, for herself and her son. To this day, she believes that it was intervention from the Spirit world which influenced the principal to change his mind and allow her to take her son from the school. Rani is also convinced that the woman at the bus stop was in fact an 'angel' who had taken human form to help her in her hour of great need.

Christine Simmons

My three small children and I were staying with my mother in her bungalow close to the sea. It was early in the morning, very quiet, and I was listening to the waves breaking on the nearby rocky beach. No-one in the house was moving, but I was wondering drowsily if it was time to get the children up. My watch was on a high chest-of-drawers beside my bed and, though I felt I ought to get up and see what the time was, I was too warm and comfortable to make the effort.

Suddenly I seemed to be suspended above the chest-of-drawers. I looked down at my watch and it was half past seven. I was really frightened and thought, 'This is a judgement on me for being too lazy to get out of bed and check the time.' Instantly I found myself back in bed. I got out immediately, picked up my watch, and, sure enough, it was half past seven!

I didn't tell anyone about this at the time as I considered they would think

I was mad, but years later I did tell a friend. She was unsurprised. 'This can happen,' she said, 'when you are relaxed but concentrating.'

However, it certainly isn't an experience that I would deliberately seek!

Beryl Spence

This happened to me in the early days when I was just realising that there is more to life than the temporal earthly state which we seem to inhabit: that we actually live in a spiritual universe and that, with the right frame of mind we can actually become aware of this dimension. Probably at that time I would not have put it quite like that. I was just becoming more open to the ideas which seemed to be flooding my way, from books, from the people I met, and, because of my increasing involvement in meditation, from the intuitions and insights that began to enrich my life. It was exciting and new, compulsive and irresistible, and hinted of a vastness which I could hardly begin to comprehend.

One day I was driving over to visit my parents. Although it was a much frequented trunk road, it wasn't a busy time of day and I was – as they say - bombing along in the fast lane, overtaking. Suddenly I found myself looking down at the top of my head, through the car roof. I continued driving without any sense of fear or even unease. It just seemed very natural. I knew I would be safe and that I would get to my parents' place without any problem. And, what has always remained in my mind, was the feeling of inconsequence about what I was doing, and where I was going. It didn't matter; it wasn't important. I was in a place or state which rendered everything we do here as unreal. The reality was/is within the raised level of consciousness in which, briefly, I found myself.

This was well before I became a Quaker, but after I had drifted away from the Church of England and at a time when I was spiritually searching, and coming to understand that God, or whatever we choose to call It, is not contained within any one religion or creed. That, in fact, It contains all of them, and none. All disciplines contain some of the truth, and serve to point the way, but Truth itself is beyond any of them.

There have been other, similar moments but none as striking and memorable as that one. And even after all these years, I can still recall the feeling of utter peace and safety that enveloped me, and the sheer *knowing*.

Rosalind Smith

The source of the following is a Mrs Doris Mason. The text was written by her son, **Don Mason**, *Emeritus Professor of Immunology, Oxford University, and is an extract from his book,* Science, Mystical Experiences and Religious Belief, *published by Sessions of York in 2006. The book is now out of print but the text can be found on the QFAS website.*

Don writes, 'My mother was very psychic and I was privileged throughout my childhood to be aware that there is more in reality than that which is accessible by the five senses. This account is but one example of my mother's gift.'

There are clearly cases of the acquisition of information by paranormal means that may involve telepathy or seeing-at-distance or both. One such example is as follows.

Towards the end of WWII my mother was consulted by a middle-aged woman who said very little but who gave her a small brown paper parcel. The use of such an item seems to focus the attention of the psychic on the person most closely associated with the article in question. During the séance that followed my mother said that the brown paper parcel contained a football jersey and that it belonged to a young man who was very keen on sports. She went on to say that the young man had been christened 'John, but everyone calls him Jack'. My mother then said she was experiencing a sensation of flying 'but not in an aeroplane'. This feeling puzzled her but she could give no explanation for it. Finally, she remarked that she felt very cold and she interpreted this to mean that the young man was dead.

Happily it transpired that this interpretation was erroneous but all the facts that my mother gave at the time were correct. Although several of these facts were known to my mother's visitor, who introduced herself after the sitting as Jack's mother, those relating to her son's immediate military deployment were not. These became known to my mother's visitor only after her son returned from the war. The sensation of flying, but not in an aeroplane, arose because the young man was a paratrooper who had taken part in the raid on Arnhem in September 1944. This raid involved the use of gliders towed behind aeroplanes to transport the paratroopers to the target area. The football jersey was a silk one and it had been wrapped up very tightly so as to give no clue as to its nature. Also, as was learned afterwards, the sensation of cold was entirely accurate. At the time Jack was in a ditch, taking cover from the German attack and he was physically cold.

If telepathy was the sole explanation here, then it would have to involve the acquisition of information from both the paratrooper's mother and her son. Alternatively, seeing-at-a distance could account for my mother learning of the contents of the brown paper parcel but would not account for the sensation of cold that my mother associated with it.

Don Mason

I know that I am not my body but in it, as I once had an out of body experience after a traffic accident, when I watched the ambulance coming and the crowd gathering from above. It was a beautiful, joyful sense of freedom and it was with some reluctance that I came back into my body (and faced all the drama and pain).

Also, sitting beside my dying Mother many years ago, reaching utter despair and crying out to God to show me what to do, I had the most beautiful spiritual experience of my life. I will try to find the words: We were both wrapped in an ocean of love, joy, peace. Everything, even this hideous accident, made sense and was contained in the certainty that all is well. There was an absolute knowing that there is no separation: all is one.

I am sure there is 'something more' after we die and am unafraid and content to wait. I could even say that I look forward to death as I am curious to discover what will happen next.

Diana Lampen

In the early days of Quaker Fellowship for Afterlife Studies, David Hodges, a biological scientist and university lecturer for over 30 years, undertook the compilation of a bibliography and discussion of the main sources of evidence supporting the survival of death. It was a huge task but, in 2004, the result of his researches appeared in book form under the title: Do We Survive Death?

As more and more new books were published it became out of date, and is now out of print. It was, and remains, a unique and valuable resource for anyone wishing to study the subject.

To represent David's own position at the end of his researches, we have chosen some passages from a section headed, 'Personal Conclusions'.

The mass of evidence supporting survival is composed of accounts of many different events and investigations. Taken separately, almost all of these can be individually criticised by the sceptically minded in one or more ways.

The intention of the critics is to show that there are flaws in the observation or interpretation of the event, so that any conclusion supporting survival or other paranormal explanation must be ruled out. However, when taken together as a whole, for me, the evidence forms an integrated, coherent and very considerable foundation, underpinning the concept of survival. It also provides a justification for the belief in survival which the great majority of humanity has held for millennia. Nevertheless, however strong the evidence for survival appears to be, it must be accepted that there is, as yet, no absolutely incontrovertible evidence which provides an overwhelming case in its favour.

. . . The most important question in life, because so much hangs on the answer, is this:

> *Which view of the universe, the spiritual approach or the material approach, best describes reality and which is redundant?*

I suggest that the evidence for survival, which is partly outlined in this bibliography, provides a sound basis for an answer in favour of the spiritual approach to life.

. . . acceptance of the concept of survival, with all that goes with it, provides us with a positive, purposeful context within which to live our lives. If we turn out to be wrong we will have lived happier, more meaningful lives but will go quietly into oblivion. On other hand, if we are right, the whole of eternity is open to us and we will have placed our feet firmly on the path of return to the Source from which all and everything comes.

David Hodges

It was cold, the early morning streets frost-rimed, as we made our way to the Maundy Thursday said Eucharist at York Minster. The previous evening we had been there for the sung evensong which had seemed more like a performance of sacred music than a service of worship. The Minster was bustling with tourists, many taking photographs despite the polite requests not to do so; milling and spilling pervaded the air with a restlessness that disturbed the atmosphere and made the act of worship difficult. The music was good and I enjoyed that.

As we walked, the streets were empty, quiet and still, and it was as though we were the only people around. I quietly opened the side door to go to the side chapel for the service, and felt the enormity of the silence, a waiting, waiting, as the building had done for a thousand years. My feet took me, hushed, noiselessly, not to the side chapel but into the main cathedral where it was breathtakingly beautiful. The sun shone through the stained-glass windows. I gazed in awe; saw much that was missed in the movement of the previous evening. I was totally alone and stood in wonderment. A gentle feeling washed over me and I became aware of a sense of benign presence. It was as if all the worship ever offered there, all the people who had come, like me, to offer worship was absorbed and held in the air, in the fabric of the building. I hung my head in shame. I had so little to bring to this place. I knew that I should worship with every particle of my being but had so little there, one single drop when an ocean was not enough.

As I stood there ashamed of the paucity of my offering, all sense of self, time and place slipped away. The 'I' no longer existed and was absorbed into a golden Light of love unimaginable. It was within me; I was within it. I felt accepted and that the worship that I was bringing was enough, it was real and was indeed enough; the molecule that I brought was added to the whole. How long I stood there I do not know. I had been in a place where time was irrelevant. The moment was broken by the soft footfall of an Anglican nun moving swiftly towards the side chapel, seeming almost like an image, a ghost from long ago. Suddenly there, jolting me back to myself, was my husband, John, asking what I thought that I was doing. He had to come looking for me because I was supposed to meet him at the chapel, I was to hurry or we'd be late.

And so it was that we went to the service. It was the familiar rite; I said the well-known and at that time, the well-loved words. I waited patiently for the golden Light that I had just seen and felt; that presence of love, to pervade the chapel. The words distracted me. I could not feel the spirit. Finally I came to understand what was for me, the meaning of worship, where all sense of self, time and place are irrelevant, and where love is all, and acceptance, of you, a human just as you are, is important. I saw that to love God is all that is asked. I no longer had to say the words, follow the rules. All I had to do was love God and seek to come that close again. That Maundy Thursday was the beginning of the end for me of being an Anglican. I found the Spirit in a gathered Quaker Meeting, in walking the hills, sitting beside the waves. This Spirit is there everywhere and is there for everyone.

Robin Goodman

To write about a shard of eternity within the breast is to contemplate 'other' matters. Mist evaporating in sunrise, water shaken from a dog's coat, firelight – all transitory glimpses of an inexpressible form, adding richness and significance to the day. The act of description obscures more than it reveals. The worm in the apple turns out to be life abounding and a cause for joy; sharing comes into this.

I am in my seventieth year. Just over half my life ago someone knocked on the clear plastic pane of my back door. I was loading the washing machine and didn't want distraction or the baby to be woken. There was no one there. Perhaps it was next door; no one there either, no close neighbour on the other side. It came again and I recognised a tale from tradition and knew that I must welcome the 'stranger' if they brought peace and love – and that was that.

A few nights later, sometime during the deeps of sleep, I found myself in an octagonal room at the top of a high tower. The view was blue sky all around and a few white clouds. In the centre of the room, a great, old round table with an abundantly loaded fruit bowl. A man in monk's habit welcomed me warmly. He approached from the left, signifying a past relationship, and indeed he was familiar, but I don't know from where or when. All he said was, 'These unfinished tasks, they have a negative drag.' We had agreed to do something that I had forgotten, so I made no reply – and that was that. Life pottered on for a few weeks. My youngest early walker didn't fall from window ledges or garden walls. The other two got on with sums, reading and playing horses in the street. Once more during sleep – it never seems like dreaming – I became aware of floating, naked, at the farthest reaches of my consciousness, stars blazed all around, above and below and I drifted in measureless peace.

Then I noticed movement far below and to one side, coming towards me very fast. It was a vast globe, composed of countless beings, increasing in brightness into the centre. I knew I could not look into that brilliant nucleus and shielded my eyes as the entity noticed me and sent out a wave of joy, love and recognition. It knew me and loved me and with great good humour changed course rather than obliterate me. That altered direction caught me in a cosmic wind, a flick of God's cloak, that spun me back into my bed. I was as winded as if I had done a handstand and landed on my back, and I rolled out of bed onto hands and knees, gasping. My husband wasn't too impressed by the commotion.

I don't know whether I slept again that night – certainly I made tea and pondered. Perhaps the biggest comprehension was that God is not one but many, that this entity is, like us, a process, and it also aspires. It is not a final destination, but another beginning. This was the start of an ongoing inner reality which still continues in a less dramatic way. It took a decade or so to establish a way of being that is akin to conversations with a dear friend. Usually the friend takes the lead, but will respond if asked in a firm voice. I cannot go against directions and am required to respond fairly promptly to urgings, and I have found forms for those responses; sometimes by painting, sometimes poetry or, as here, a written piece. This mystery demands attending, as worker bees attend the queen, but defies concrete definition. I am less sure now of what it means than before all the 'dreams' began, except to say, mistrust finite explanations: it is larger than we can comprehend. It's the grounding that's important, attempting to make something that did not exist before, with this rarely captured 'oneness' at its core.

Liz Silk

Here is an experience which came early in the life of a new Quaker.

There were discussion and worship-sharing groups at my meeting when I first arrived, but there wasn't any forum in which I could exchange ideas and experiences and hear back what other people thought or had experienced, because a part of the format was the open listening and silent space, and commenting upon other people's contributions wasn't allowed. I couldn't find a place outside the main meeting where that sort of exchange was allowed.

As it happened, shortly after I started attending meeting I had a very puzzling experience which I was struggling to process. I was walking down the high street with my daughter in her pram, not thinking particularly spiritual thoughts at all, when suddenly I was out of my body, high above the high street, and I experienced a bliss, which I knew immediately was the experience of being one with God and yet myself. Then I realised I was one with *everything* and felt deep love for everything I could see. I remember feeling deep love for the tiles on the top of the roof, which I was above, while at the same time being surprised that it wasn't just animate beings which triggered this overwhelming love, it was everything in the material world. It answered a question I had had in my mind for a long time, about the possibility of retaining an identity while being a part of God.

I have come to realise over the years that we are all made of God - indeed that there is nothing else for things to be made from - but that is more of an intellectual processing of the information I received on that day from that experience, and not something I instinctively knew.

I didn't know how to share that experience, and really I have only just begun to do so properly. I did share it once in a Quaker Universalist meeting and was met with a very negative response (clearly Quaker Universalists do not observe the strict rules which were imposed by my meeting on worship sharing) when the man next to me said: 'that's not an unusual experience, you're not so special, lots of people have experienced exactly the same!' It wasn't a very kind comment and wasn't very kindly said, and it was years before I tried to share the experience again.

I have come to realise that many Quakers feel that discussing or telling other people about their beliefs is somehow "influencing" the other person, and they think of this as a negative thing, akin to trying to convert the other to their way of thinking. I was wanting to learn from others - throughout my life I have felt led to information, and guided, and I didn't see hearing other people's experiences as a negative thing at all - I wanted to know, wanted to learn through other people. I certainly had the experience on many occasions of feeling that someone in meeting was led to say exactly the thing I needed to hear, but I felt in need of a creative collaboration, I suppose a synergy or exchange would express it better.

I have worked on creative projects where I feel that the sharing and collaboration made the project more than the sum of its parts, and I felt sure that was also possible for spiritual life as well. There are some things which I have been convinced of by intellect - when I first came to Quakers, it started like that, but then I began to feel that I had actually always been a Quaker, but hadn't realised that was what I was. That sort of recognition I think of as a heart knowing, not an intellectual head knowing. When you experience something which seems outside the realm of the normal material world, you don't have to be convinced intellectually that something real has happened, you just know.

Fee Berry

Are you able to contemplate your death and the death of those closest to you? Accepting the fact of death, we are freed to live more fully. In bereavement, give yourself time to grieve. When others mourn, let your love embrace them.

Advices and queries: 30

2.18

Be still and cool in thy own mind and spirit from thy own thoughts, and then thou wilt feel the principle of God to turn thy mind to the Lord God, whereby thou wilt receive his strength and power from whence life comes, to allay all tempests, against blusterings and storms. That is it which moulds up into patience, into innocency, into soberness, into stillness, into stayedness, into quietness, up to God, with his power.

George Fox , 1658

(Quaker Faith & Practice, 1995.)

An Eternity Before Us

This article was published in The Friend, *9.1.2015. It is included in this Anthology to show just how necessary the work of Quaker Fellowship for Afterlife Studies is in supporting those Friends who have found it difficult or impossible to share their spiritual/psychic experiences in their meetings. It highlights the distress and sense of isolation Friends may feel in these circumstances.*

Recently I received a phone call from a Friend in distress. The message was typical of many I have received over the years, and I feel that perhaps it is time to speak out. The distress was caused because the Friend concerned was unable to speak openly to anyone in his Meeting about an experience he had had: the experience of contact from a recently deceased and much loved partner. The fact that such contacts frequently take place after the death of someone who has been very close, seems, unfortunately, not to be understood by the majority of Friends, which mirrors the situation in society generally. But the Religious Society of Friends is a body which recognizes a spiritual dimension to life and we should surely be more open minded on the subject. Early Friends were. The existence of God and Heaven, was a natural part of their faith, indeed the basis of their faith, as was communication with those in the next life.

The following is recounted in George Fox's Book of Miracles: "George Fox's mother died in 1674, when Fox was in Worcester gaol, and was prevented from visiting her. When the letter about her death reached him, he was grieved, but – 'When my spirit had gotten through I saw her in the resurrection and the life, everlastingly with me, and father in the flesh also.'"

Quaker Fellowship for Afterlife Studies has been in existence since 2000. During this time we have studied the subject of the existence of an afterlife from many angles, and begun an exploration into the huge amount of evidence which exists. In 2004, David Hodges, member of Ashford QM, a biological scientist and university lecturer, compiled a reference book: *Do we Survive Death?: A descriptive bibliography and Discussion on the Evidence Supporting Survival,* which lists and describes many of the books which have been written on the subject, and gives details of their authors.

Paranormal experience (or spiritual/psychic experience as QFAS members prefer to call it) has always been part of human existence. At present, sadly, in academia, scientific materialism prevails, and such experience is frequently denigrated and dismissed in a thoroughly unscientific way.

It appears that many scientists are unaware that since its foundation in 1882, the Society for Psychical Research has had many distinguished presidents including two Nobel Prize winners, several Fellows of the Royal Society, many professors of Physics, Philosophy and Chemistry, a Bishop, a future Prime Minister and a founder member of the League of Nations. In fact, many distinguished scientists have studied the subject and been convinced by what they have discovered. What is not generally realised is that to come out in support of the genuine nature of the evidence is extremely detrimental to a scientist's career.

Retirement allows freedom of expression! William Crookes, eminent man of science, knighted by Queen Victoria in 1897, made a three year study of mediums and mediumship from 1870-73. When he published his positive findings he was derided by his colleagues who threatened to deprive him of his Fellowship of the Royal Society. Fearful for his reputation and future career, Crookes resumed his normal scientific work and went quiet on the subject that had consumed his interest for so long.

After his retirement he served a term as President of the Society for Psychical Research, and said in 1917, just two years before his death: 'I have never had any occasion to change my mind on the subject. I am perfectly satisfied with what I have said in earlier days. It is quite true that a connection has been set up between this world and the next.'

Sir Arthur Conan Doyle (doctor of medicine) and Sir Oliver Lodge (physicist, and principal of Birmingham University) were also early psychical researchers, and convinced of the genuine nature of much of the communication with those in the afterlife, either directly or through mediumship (and this long before they lost sons in WWI). Both wrote extensively on the subject.

In our own times there have been two Quakers amongst those courageous enough to publish the truth as they saw it. Don Mason, member of Witney QM, Emeritus Professor of Cellular Immunology, Oxford University, wrote *Science, Mystical Experience and Religious Belief*, in 2006. Don argues convincingly for the existence of an afterlife drawing on a lifetime of experience, and as part of his concluding remarks writes: '…I do believe we have an eternity before us…' In 2008, Robert Anderson, a New Zealand Quaker, with a PhD in science education and a combined honours degree in physics and chemistry, wrote *You Can't Die for the Life of You!*, an account of his forty year plus study of death and the paranormal. Bob's title is typical of the style in which he vigorously expresses himself, energetically piling up the evidence in support of his case!

If human beings do survive death (whether expecting to or not) what more natural than that we should wish to communicate the fact to our nearest and dearest who are left behind in a state of grief? Could we please show more consideration to the bereaved people who may see, hear or vividly dream about their loved ones? They long to share their precious experience with their Quaker Friends. What could be more natural? And it may not be a delusion that they are suffering. It may be an actual, joyful event.

(Books referred to:
Hodges, David. *Do we Survive Death? A Descriptive Bibliography and Discussion on the Evidence Supporting Survival*, ISBN 0-9546122-0-5.
Mason, Don. *Science, Mystical Experience and Religious Belief*, 2006, Sessions, ISBN 185072-357-5. Anderson, Robert. *You Can't Die for the Life of You!* 2008, ISBN 978-0-473-13157-9 (published privately and not currently available in the UK).

Angela Howard

In November 1987, I saw the BBC documentary *14 Days in May* about the execution of a young black man, Edward Earl Johnson. Through the film, I began corresponding with another Death Row prisoner in Mississippi, Sam Johnson (no relation to Edward Earl).

Sam was the second Sam Johnson to come into my life. The first was the Master of my college (Queen's) at Melbourne University, Raynor Johnson, in the early 1960s. Being Dr Johnson, he was inevitably referred to by the students as "Sam", in honour of Dr Samuel Johnson.

Raynor Johnson was a world authority on mysticism and psychical research, and had written a number of distinguished books in this field. The most notable of these was *The Imprisoned Splendour*. "Sam" gave lectures on the subject in college. These were a wonderful synthesis of mystical experience, the world's great faiths, science (Raynor was himself a distinguished physicist) and teachings from literature and poetry. His teachings influenced me greatly. I also got to know Raynor well in his and my final year, 1964, when I was president of the student body.

I wrote to Sam in Mississippi early on about the previous "Sam" Johnson in my life and sent him a copy of *The Imprisoned Splendour*. I mentioned too that after Sam had retired I had stayed in touch with him, but that now the title of "Master", as we all addressed him, had taken on a new and deeper meaning. I noted too that Raynor Johnson had died in May 1987 (a week after Edward Earl Johnson was executed). Sam responded warmly to the book and we discussed it in our letters.

A year after I began writing to Sam I decided that I had to go out and meet him. A week before I was due to fly out, I was sitting in my study reading a book about the strange psychic experiences of a Norfolk doctor, Ian Pearce, who had tragically lost a daughter at a young age. It was the kind of book that made me sit back and reflect from time to time.

All of a sudden, during one of these pauses, I "saw" Raynor Johnson before me. I do not mean physically but with my mind's eye. The image was however very vivid and distinct: I remember noting that Sam was much younger than I had known him.

The apparition then said, 'Shake Sam by the hand, and tell him that the Master sends his love.' Although the visual image was unusually clear, I could not help wondering whether my mind was playing tricks, and found myself replying, 'Master, you were a scientist and always demanded proof. I cannot possibly go out to Mississippi and give Sam that message unless I have proof that it has come from you.'

The being before me then said, 'Go to the bookshelf and take down my book and look at page 157.' Feeling a bit of an idiot, and convinced that my mind was working overtime, I took down *The Imprisoned Splendour*. Turning to page 157 I had expected some weighty or particularly beautiful philosophical passage. Instead, it was a factual account of some obscure experiments on precognition and retrocognition conducted half a century before by one Whately Carrington. By now the vision had faded and I thought, 'There you are, it's your mind playing tricks,' and returned to the book by Ian Pearce.

Ten minutes later I came to a new chapter and there was an account of the Whately Carrington experiments (the only other time I had ever come across a reference to these experiments). I leant back and said, 'Thank you Master, I have my answer.'

Note that the experiments were about precognition. Such a neat, scientific and slightly humorous "proof" in Raynor had "precognized" that I should be soon reading this passage. That was entirely consistent with Raynor's personality.

But the story does not end there. I went out to Mississippi the next week and duly visited Sam on Death Row. The visiting room there at that time consisted of a shed or annexe perhaps 30 feet long divided down the middle by a waist-high brick wall with above it a heavy mesh grille. It would not have been possible to shake a little finger, let alone hands.

Sam came in on the other side accompanied by a young black guard. He and Sam obviously knew each other quite well, and the guard was well disposed to Sam. I had gone in as a "paralegal", and the guard asked, 'Would you like to have the hatch opened? Do you have any papers that Sam needs to see or sign?'

Set into the grille was a solid metal hatch about a foot square. In the background Sam was nodding his head like mad. And so I said to the guard, 'Yes, that would be helpful,' and he opened the hatch.

Even then, however, it would not ordinarily have been possible for us to shake hands, as Sam was meant to be manacled to a waist-chain. But as the guard took Sam into the waiting room, he saw Sam's big smile and said, 'What's up with you, man?' - and forgot to handcuff him. Sam and I were able to reach through the hatch - and shake hands.

Needless to say I passed on Raynor's message to Sam and explained the extraordinary circumstances in which it had come about. It made a deep impression on us both, and was certainly quite an ice-breaker!

A little over 12 years later, in March 2001, Sam was dying in the hospital of the same prison. Through a friendly doctor who had known Sam for a long time, I knew that Sam was close to the end. I sent the doctor an e-mail asking him to convey the following message to Sam: 'Tell Sam that Jan shakes him by the hand and sends his love.' I told the doctor that Sam would understand the message.

Two or three days later, Sam died. Naturally, I wondered whether there might be some message from Sam. A week or so after Sam died I had a strong sense of his presence, but there was nothing tangible that I could point to as a message from him. Again, it was possible that my imagination was simply running away with me.

Then, one afternoon I needed to look something up on teletext on television and, just as I was about to switch off, came across the last few minutes of a film called *The Defiant Ones*. It was a black and white film with Tony

Curtis and Sydney Poitier as two escaped convicts who were handcuffed to one another and who, despite their differences (especially the fact that one was white and the other black), were forced to co-operate. Years before, when I had first seen the film, I had written to Sam about it. He had seen it and it had also made a considerable impression on him. We joked a little that we were like Tony Curtis and Sydney Poitier in being bound so closely together and co-operating despite our very different backgrounds.

The last few minutes of the film show the two of them running away from the police. By now they had managed to get rid of the handcuffs. Sniffer dogs are on their trail and their only hope of escape is to catch a freight train as it slows to cross a bridge. Sydney Poitier manages to get on the train, but Tony Curtis has been shot in the shoulder and can't quite make it. Sydney Poitier holds out his hand as Curtis sprints desperately beside the train. At last, they manage to clasp hands. Although Poitier is unable to haul Curtis up on to the train, and indeed jumps off so that they will be arrested together, the moment the camera zeroed in on the "handshake" between one black and one white hand, I knew unmistakably that this was Sam's message in reply.

Jan Arriens

Pat Gundrey has been having spiritual/psychic experiences for most of her life. Now in her seventies, she felt it was time to gather together some of the most memorable in a small booklet. The extract below is taken from her most unusual and sustained contact with a Quaker friend, Alex.

I had rekindled my interest in Buddhism and had been attending a weekly class and meditating regularly. On return from a retreat I heard that a good friend, Alex, had died unexpectedly. He was an attender at our Quaker meeting. On the fourth morning after his death I felt a cloudy fuzzy feeling around my head. It took me a while to remember this experience from the past. I took up a pen and his message was clear:

There's more there's more, there's much, much more. I'm surrounded by love and light.

We found it very easy to tune in to each other and were soon chatting away. The funeral was to be held in the meeting house. At the same time that I was helping to plan it I was in touch with the man to be buried, and when I was discussing the event with his daughter in the meeting house he was there with us. An hour before the funeral he was with me at the computer suggesting what I should say in the last line of my little speech and advising me not to recite the poem I intended to – he considered it maudlin.

The funeral went off well. Alex was looking forward to it and enjoyed seeing family and old friends. In the bleak hillside cemetery near his home I watched dry eyed as his coffin was lowered into the grave knowing that he was with me and we'd embarked on the adventure of understanding this extraordinary situation we found ourselves in. Eventually we could make contact without the writing and were with each other constantly.

The next week was many things – ecstatic but tricky, as we tried to accommodate our relationship into my domestic one. There were tense moments as my husband, W, seemed not to want to face up to this new take on reality. Alex and he had been friends and the three of us did discuss the situation. W's witty remarks got more and more barbed as he realised that I was taking all this seriously. He had a choice, one of us was deluded... he seemed to decide it was me. In the end I let him believe that Alex had moved on but I think he was still a bit suspicious as he said I'm much better at cryptic crosswords than I used to be!

Alex tells his story by channelling through me to the PC rather than the pen... *When I awoke shortly after my death I was outside my body and aware of it being moved from hospital to funeral parlour. I realised I must be dead and this was confirmed by weeping and wailing friends - I was quite surprised how well liked I was. I felt desperately lonely and sought out friends who I hoped I could reach. I was relieved to get through to Pat, a Quaker friend ... it was wonderful to be comforted by her. I was feeling* *lonely and confused and a bit panicky. She was so upset by my death that she realised how much she had loved me, and I had known for a while that I felt the same. It was a very strange and confusing time with mixed emotions – my overwhelming urge was to give love and be loved. I wanted to be with Pat but there was a feeling of impermanence ... a feeling that I must move on, but to where?*

There was an occasion when Pat took me to a Buddhist ceremony the purpose of which was to help the recent dead on their way. Pat was told that she shouldn't let her attachment to me hold me. Nine weeks on and we are still together – reading, listening to music, doing crosswords etc... We feel we are meant to be together as we couldn't be in real life. It feels like a precious gift we have been given, but how long will it last? When we communicate I feel present and alive, but when she is occupied doing things, I feel like a fly on the wall. And of course it is frustrating not to be able to communicate with friends we meet when I'm with her especially if I knew them well. We really are a bit glued together. She says it's like being possessed in the nicest possible way. She really is quite extraordinary because she manages to blend two worlds together. She loves us both and it is as though W and I complement each other. We chug along, a ménage a trois.

Alex did move on but he soon returned. He seemed a little different ... a bit more refined and it seemed he had lost some of his earthly persona. It was at this point that Maram, my spirit guide, introduced him/herself to me and explained that Alex and I were meant to be together to help each other on our spiritual journeys. It just feels right having this loving presence with me at all times and I feel that I function more positively in all that I am involved in. It feels like we really are two hearts beating as one ... does that make us soul mates then?

There will come a time says Rudolf Steiner when we shall have assistance in our activities on earth. The souls of those we have loved who have passed into the spiritual worlds will then live on in our consciousness. That this is not yet experienced by many is because spiritual scientific development is as yet only really beginning. It has not yet planted in souls the capacities and power that can act freely out of selfless love and love filled wisdom. The path to such an experience of the presence and help of the dead will gradually open up for many souls in future.

We may think about the dead while about our daily work; we may awaken in our hearts all the selfless love we harboured for them, and the moment will come when we have the clear conscious experience that the one who has died is helping us as if he kindled our ardour for the work we are doing, as if she or he were working through our very hands and fingers. This clear feeling, this conscious inner experience, that the spiritual influences work down from the spiritual worlds into our physical earth lives, is a fruit a living fruit, that comes to those souls who in selfless surrender, in spiritualised love, tread the path of spiritual development

Also from Steiner – A person who has died before us and whom we completely forget finds it almost impossible to reach us. The love, the constant sympathy and warmth we feel for the dead creates a path by which connection can be made with those who remain on earth. It is only over the 'bridge of love' which we build, that those who have departed earthly existence can find a connection.

It still requires a raised consciousness on the part of the earth bound to make the connection.

Pat Gundrey

Pat is happy to send a free copy of her booklet, This Much I Know, *on request. Email:* pat.gundrey@gmail.com

Part 1: Christmas Eve 2012

Even though I had caught a cold and cough on 22 December, I decided at the last minute that I should still go to the carol service with my husband in the Cathedral. The bus was late getting us into town, so we had to sprint to join the queue. There were so many waiting that we doubted we would all fit. Had we left it too late this time?

I got chatting with a couple standing in front of us. He was an American called John, and had started lecturing at Nuffield College a year ago. She was Australian, named Dianne. They lived in Suffolk and had a temporary flat in Oxford while trying to find a house here. This was their first time at a service in the Cathedral.

The queue started moving and we kept talking. Dianne was from Margaret River in Western Australia. Amazed by this, I ventured that I was from Perth, but had been living in England since 1979. Eventually we all got seated right beside the altar – our best position ever. For the first time we could see all the guest readers in the pulpit, who were normally obscured by a pillar.

It was a lovely carol service, including a French carol. I managed to sing along despite my cold. At the end of the service I spoke to Dianne and John again, gave them my card in case I could be of help with their house hunting, and said goodbye.

Part 2: Epiphany, 6 January 2013

An email arrived from Dianne today. She studied at the WA Institute of Technology (now Curtin University) with my mother in 1974. We knew her then as Di (not Dianne). Having looked at my card, she realised the family connection from my surname (I kept my name when I married) and remembered my mum's "wonderful poetry" from their creative writing class. What is even more poignant is that she is living in a flat and looking for a house now, but back then she had helped us to move from a flat to a house. This was a staggering synchronicity after 38 years. I had not recognised her, nor she me, but as I was only 10 when we had last seen each other that was less surprising!

I emailed her at once to confirm the synchronicity and called mum as well. Mum said she had dreamt of Di only the day before, which further confirmed the synchronous link. Mum said she had seen Di in a dream, but could not remember her name. She was recalling one of her old poems at the time, and Di appeared in the dream. A lovely Twelfth Night gift.

Rhonda Riachi

I was brought up surrounded by mediums and spiritual healers, but, although much influenced by Spiritualist philosophy, I never felt the need to join a Spiritualist church.

I was, therefore, surprised when, not long after I had found my spiritual home with the Quakers, I was drawn to attend my local Spiritualist church. There, one evening, a medium gave me a reading and told me that she could see a nun with me. The nun indicated that I was to become involved in the healing ministry and that I had been led to the church as part of a plan which would start to manifest itself in October. The medium then said that the nun was telling her that she had joined her Order at a very young age following great opposition and through her own persistence in overcoming it. I saw no reason why I should have been told this, little realising it was a clue to the nun's identity.

Later that summer, I visited Westminster Cathedral. There I was drawn with a strong psychic intensity to a picture of St. Therese of Lisieux, although I had never heard of her before. It was as though she was saying 'you will need to take notice of me soon.'

On 1st October, St. Therese's Feast Day, a Quaker friend asked me to a meeting of the local CFPSS group to hear a tape of a talk given by Barbara Bunce at a recent conference. He told me it concerned communications believed to have been inspired by St. Therese. I accepted his invitation and, now that I had reason to do so, decided to find out about this saint whose picture had so drawn me. I began to read St. Therese's autobiography and when I learnt of her struggle to enter Carmel at the age of 15, I knew with a sudden and astonishing inner conviction, that she was the nun who had come to me in May.

I enjoyed Barbara's talk and found the evidence as to the source of the communications very convincing. On seeing a friend, Jean, from the local Spiritualist church the following Sunday, I felt moved to tell her what I had heard. Her response was one of surprise and it astounded me too. She told me that she also had been a channel for communications seemingly from St. Therese. Her story, like Barbara's, was highly evidential. Thus, it seemed to me that I had been led to learn about the two sets of communications as though it were part of some plan, and in October, as the medium had said.

Yet, there seemed to me to be a conflict between them. Those of Barbara's talk, while accepting that other religions have truth, stressed the importance of 'pure Christianity' and of following Christ. Jean's communications, on the other hand, while giving Jesus as an example to follow, stressed that one should look for enlightenment in all the great religions. The common strand between them, however, was that, whatever one's spiritual path, one should always seek to follow the way of love. Love is the basis of St. Therese's own philosophy, and, as I was to discover, the answer to apparent conflict between the communications.

The importance of love in St. Therese's teaching was emphasized to me soon afterwards, during Quaker Meeting for Worship, when I felt an overwhelming command to pick up a Bible and open it at random. I did so reluctantly since I had already sat down and the Bibles were on the other side of the room but the feeling was so strong that I had to obey it. When I opened the Bible, I found myself reading St. Paul's famous teaching on love in 1 Corinthians, Chapter 13. It was this passage which had inspired

St. Therese to make love her own vocation. I was sure I had been led to this text and was confirmed in this belief when, that very evening, Jean was inspired against her own plans to read one of St. Therese's communications based on the same passage while officiating at the Spiritualist church service.

Not long after this, again at the Spiritualist church, I heard Jean read one of her communications where Therese urged us to follow Jesus' example of love and humility. The following day, I suddenly received an inner command to listen again to the communications in Barbara's talk. I had acquired a tape of it to which I rarely listened since it had proved faulty and constantly jammed when played and had to be released before continuing. On this occasion, too, the tape kept jamming during Barbara's introduction and I would have given up but for the irresistible urge to go on. At the point where Barbara began to read the addresses themselves, the tape suddenly started to run smoothly – something quite unprecedented – and continued to do so until the end of the last communication.

Hearing these addresses again, with their strong emphasis on the love of Christ, so soon after hearing Jean's communication about Him, I realized there was no conflict after all between the two sets of addresses. The essential message in both was the same. We should seek truth from wherever it may come and not limit our search to any one religion but, above all, we should follow the way of love, as demonstrated in the life and teaching of Jesus Christ. This is the way of 'pure Christianity'.

This was confirmed shortly afterwards when Jean herself attended a sitting with a medium. A nun came through saying she brought roses (flowers famously linked with St. Therese) and confirmed that she was the one who had communicated through Jean. She then said that her message was always one of love and that she herself could 'claim no virtue except through the love of Christ' whose 'Victory is absolute.'

Over the next few weeks, new understandings came to me, often in circumstances as though I was being guided. I saw that Christ came to manifest the power of Divine Love and in doing so demonstrated the ultimate Victory of Love over human adversity.

I felt I had been through a kind of training and, just as the nun had told me through the medium at the local spiritualist church, I soon found myself called to the healing ministry as a way to follow Christ's example and be a channel for the power of Divine Love. Opportunities then opened up for me to do this and I have now worked as a healer for many years, first with the National Federation of Spiritual Healers, and more recently with the Friends Fellowship of Healing.

I shall always be grateful for the inspiration I received through my encounter with St. Therese of Lisieux.

Cherry Simpkin

When my twin brother died suddenly and in rather tragic circumstances late in 2012, I knew that I would need to try and make contact with him as soon as I could, striking a balance between received wisdom about the desirability of waiting, and my own need. The College of Psychic Studies (CPS) advises leaving it for six months in cases of bereavement before consulting a sensitive. I did not feel I could wait that long, but I did wait as long as I could – which turned out to be just over 12 weeks.

I chose one of the CPS practitioners specialising in proof of survival after death, and the one whom I felt drawn to. (Was it a coincidence that this sensitive turned out to be a fraternal twin himself, with a female twin, just like us?) . It is also worth mentioning that before the appointment arrived, and starting shortly after Roger's death, a number of electrical disturbances had occurred - TV remotes not working at all, and then OK, ditto my iPad (and it definitely wasn't the battery), lights flickering at home, and so forth. Apparently, this is quite a common phenomenon when people have passed over, although I'm not sure why this should be so...

The appointment day of 30th January 2013 duly came and I went to the CPS headquarters in Kensington, took delivery of the CD I had ordered, and gave it to the practitioner, AK, to put in the machine. The consultation started as soon as I walked in the room, with a stream of information, most of it accurate, about other people, including my mother and father. This included pretty convincing physical detail, but I wasn't here primarily for this. Then, two thirds of the way through the session, it seemed perhaps that my brother was there, waiting, and described as middle aged (it's true that he tended to look a bit younger than his (then) 66 years).

But all doubt as to who it was went when AK went on to name him, and not just that, but in the very phrase by which he usually announced himself on the phone (it's Roger) and the official date of his death (5th November) – was it significant? However, AK described the fireworks associated with that date, and being let off by Roger, as primarily a sense of Roger celebrating his *release* from this world and his arrival in the next. AK also went on to describe Roger as dancing around, twirling his hands, in celebration, a very characteristic movement of his. It was also the case that my brother had told me that he wanted to die, several times, but he was also a devoted Catholic, and would therefore find it completely against his creed deliberately to take his own life. His resolution to his difficulties in life and this dilemma, conscious or not, was to become gradually addicted to alcohol, until his whole life revolved around it, and he gradually became more and more ill and reclusive. Ultimately it was alcohol which ended his life, through acute alcohol intoxication, whereby the automatic nervous system was so depressed that it "forgot" to breathe.

AK then asked why he saw Roger clutching a glass of wine very tightly, and followed this up by asking if Roger had died in tragic circumstances. In fact the circumstances were sufficiently tragic, but not actually suicide, (the coroner ultimately determining the cause of death as "alcohol dependent misuse").

AK went on to describe Roger (accurately) as someone who was less fortunate than me, whose problems had finally overwhelmed him here, and he couldn't cope any more. But because we were virtually at the end of the 45 minute session, there was little time to say more, and I left with my CD, feeling I had actually made contact with my brother, very happy that we were in touch and that he was at peace and enjoying his new life.

I didn't bother to make notes on the train home, because, after all, I had a CD of the complete session. And because life was hectic at that point, it was only a few days later that I sat down to play the CD recording and go through what had happened in detail. I tried the CD out on two players and then two computers, to absolutely no avail. Then the truth struck me that the CD was blank and that my session had not been recorded at all.
Naturally enough, I was pretty distraught to find I had no record of this hugely important spirit communication. Later on that evening, I sent an email to AK's website, saying that the CD was blank and that I hadn't bothered to make detailed notes because of having the CD, and what did he think I should do? Back next day came two emails, the first saying that he was extremely puzzled at this very rare event, and offering me another (free) session and CD the following week if I could make it. The second email said that AK had been thinking about the session and remembered bringing in Roger towards the end. AK had come to the conclusion that Roger had a great deal more to say to me, and that this was why the session had not recorded properly.

So back I went on 6th February 2013 to the same room in the CPS, and had my second session with AK. Once again, the CD was inserted into the machine, and then we were off. Roger was, apparently, there immediately, and this time, virtually the whole session was from and about Roger, his life, and our early life together, relayed to AK by Roger himself. I can best describe it as having all the characteristics of the "Life Review" we hear that we undergo after death, only this time, I was privileged to share Roger's own life review, which brought me in also, because we had been so very close from the earliest days in the womb.

The review was unsparingly honest, I would have been more lenient I think had I been doing the evaluating. It touched on our relationship from our earliest childhood, his later difficulties and misfortunes, the part played by his own nature, his relationship to alcohol and also much (completely accurate) detail about his temperament, characteristic movements, stressing his own responsibility for some of what had happened to him. Not a word struck a false note, and I have no doubt that I was in touch with his spirit. (It was just like talking to him through an interpreter). Now he is, I was assured, happy in the "Halls of Learning", and completely free of alcohol. (That assurance meant a lot to me.)

He was, apparently, present at his own funeral and enjoyed it very much. (And so he should have done. It was magnificent, and I and his friends took a deal of trouble with the music and singers, etc.) A recurring note of sadness, however, was that he wished that he had made more of his life... and that he wanted me to think of him at his very best, when he had the whole of his life to look forward to - in other words, in his late teens, the age he was for one of the two photographs we used in the funeral service leaflet. He also assured me, through AK, that he would meet me when I die, as he would not be coming back into another life here on earth for a long time. There was also a lot more detail about my life which need not concern us here.

I went home on the train again, only this time, I wrote notes of as much as I could remember of the session as soon as I could, not quite trusting to the CD technology. Later that same evening, I sat down to try out the CD recording. And once again, I tried it out on several CD playing devices at home, two CD players and then, my computer. Again, nothing. As a last resort, I took the CD to Ruth's room, and tried it out on her computer.

It so happened that in Ruth's room, a framed photo of Roger snapped by me a few years ago, hung from her shelf. (It was the photo we had used for the front cover of the funeral service.) Just as I was starting to say to Ruth, "It's no good, there's nothing there, just like the other one", she cried out "Look!", and pointed to this photo of Roger above me and to my right. I then looked and we both saw that *the photo and frame was rocking from side to side, throbbing or vibrating strongly. This continued for several minutes while we said, in wonder, well, it's Roger...* There was absolutely no way the vibration could have been caused by a draught of air, or any mechanical or natural means that we could see. It just wasn't that kind of movement. It was a movement which was purposeful and entirely deliberate. Nothing like that had happened before, nor has it since. *We are convinced that it was Roger, doing his best to communicate with us that he was alive, and here, and that it was his doing that we did not have a recording of my session.*

I think that he simply did not wish there to be a record, having shared such highly personal details with me. He may have been happy to share with me in person, but had not wanted a record. Alternatively, he may have planned it so that he could present what was, to us both, highly convincing proof of survival, and maybe this was his primary motive. Certainly in our younger days, he and I had speculated on survival and, I think, talked of coming back and trying to make contact with each other.

The next day I communicated what had happened to AK. He expressed great interest, and promised to try and record for me on a third CD as much of the session as he could recall, I think with Roger's help. This he duly did, and sent me the third CD with some 13 minutes or so of material on it. He said that he had found it extremely difficult to do, without a sitter, and also, very exhausting, so had to stop there.

I feel great gratitude to the medium for his superb communication with Roger and others in spirit, and also for the painstaking attempts he made to ensure that I did end up with some record of what had transpired.

So where I am now with all this? Well, I feel very lucky to have had these experiences. I am now as certain as I can be, while still on this earth, that I have been in touch with Roger's spirit, that we are, after all, spiritual beings living our life on this earth plane, that there is meaning and purpose all around us, and that all we do or fail to do, *matters*. I also want to study and learn more of the nature of reality and truth, both to prepare myself and to contribute as much as I can while I am here, to and through the life which is lived through me and through others.

Tina Day

In 1979 when I was 44 I had a Near Death Experience (NDE). Apart from completely changing my life, this experience also gave me insights about what it will mean to die and what death is, and how life is a preparation for dying well – for having a "a good death" by living life to the full.

I have written elsewhere about my life before the NDE happened, about the changes I made as a result of it, and the values and beliefs I "received" during it. I have also previously described the actual out of body experience (OBE) and of being in the Light and so on.

In this account I wish to try to explain what I learnt during the NDE – i.e. what I seemed to be being taught. I have not been able to do this before because the communication was word-less. That is I "received" knowledge *without language*. I did not *hear* anything. No-one spoke to me. It now feels important, however, twenty-two years later, to try to share – to pass on to others, the material which I received.

Although I learnt something (i.e. was taught it), it was as if I have always known it but had forgotten; or that the knowledge had previously been in little fragmented bits so unavailable to me. So it was as if I was being reminded and re-connected in order that the knowledge could become integrated and consolidated within me. It seemed it was therefore about me, myself, no longer being fragmented (even though at the time I was above my body!) but confirming instead that I was a joined-up whole-body, mind, feelings and spirit, because I always am "my true essence".

The communication happened all at once and spontaneously like an "ah-ha" experience. Like a sudden insight – a Gestalt. However, paradoxically, there seemed to be all the time in the world so that I felt I understood about eternity and infinity. I was very happy lingering there, and taking it all in – eager to absorb what I was learning (yet not being striving or ambitious, as I usually am with learning). It was relaxed and peaceful so I could just let it sweep over me and through me.

It was not like receiving intellectual knowledge but more like being enveloped in Love. I was in the presence of Love, and Love was doing the communicating. A huge-Abundance was being re-triggered in me. I knew it was all about my becoming the Love that I had always been (but had forgotten) and about my being able to manifest the Compassion that is my true nature (but of which I had been unaware).

The communication seemed to contain "all that there is to know, ever". I received all the answers to all the big questions – was able to fathom all mysteries. There was no more "fear of the unknown", no more disturbance, illness or chaos. Instead everything was suddenly very clear – I had become a Huge Clarity and Wholesomeness. Again I was in the presence of the "clear-whole" who was the communicator. And I was realizing that in my true-essence I am this Whole, Clarity, Love, Abundance, Compassion and all that was being conveyed to me. I am One with it all. So although I have now forgotten most of the details of this "knowledge", a sort of précis has remained ever since. All is One, All is Whole, and I need to just "be".

During the communication, which was a gradual realization but happened, nevertheless, as a complete whole, spontaneously, I became – "fully, consciously aware". This very alert, very clear, and very intentioned state has remained available ever since. I can become "willing and witting with my antennae aquiver", as I call it, whenever I need to be, or am guided to be. Thus I have a way of accessing where I was in my NDE. I can again become tuned-in, able to wait quietly to make the right decision, listening to inner promptings – choosing wisely because I am being guided, or channelled, by Cosmic-Wisdom or Universal-Intuition - two names I now have for God.

Much later, after the NDE, when as a result of it I had been led to become a Quaker, I realised that this was a "change of consciousness" state. It is that state which is accessed in a ministry or when meditating, healing or discerning the will of the Holy Spirit, what Quakers call "leadings".

One of the things I came to understand during the communication, was that there are no dualities and no reductionism. (I did not then know these terms.) So that these are person-made (earthly) distortions of how things really are – the Truth. So I learnt that there is, no either heaven or earth, no either matter or spirit, and so on. Instead it is "both/and", not "either/or". We are each a Whole-Oneness with all other creatures, persons, plants and the Earth, as well as being a Whole-One-ness with the spirit world. It is a seamless completeness.

I learnt that I am on a spiritual journey in eternity and infinity. At present my earthly, bodily, part of this journey started in the spirit-world which nevertheless is "The Whole". I realized, during the communication of the NDE, that I had become incarnated with "a meaning and purpose" to complete on Earth. I have tasks to fulfil before I can leave my body, to again become pure spirit. These tasks may take several life-times where I move in and out of Earth but am "be"-ing in the Whole, always in the here-and-now.

So, even whilst on the Earth, I am (and each of us is) the "Whole-in-the-part", the Whole within my own individuality. We are not each just "a *part* of the Whole" but also each *The Whole* in our true essence, the part that can move between Earth and the spirit world and which is independent of the body yet can use the body, mind and feelings as a vehicle. This Whole-Essence is what I now call my Higher-Self or the Inner-Divinity, or what Quakers call the "that-of-God-within". So, I believe it is synonymous with what I now mean by the Immanent-God, immanent *in* the Whole, *as* the Whole.

After my NDE, I was led to do my Psychosynthesis training. This allowed me to fully integrate this knowledge and make practical use of it – helping others to realize their wholeness and to learn how to transcend dualities by holding the opposites together until a synthesis is found (a both/and). So I now sometimes call God "Polarities-in-Synthesis".

The above is an attempt to describe the gist of the communication I received. I will now attempt to describe "The Tugging".

When the communication was completed, I experienced a tugging. On the one hand I yearned to stay where I was in eternal and infinite peace, knowledge, love and joy. On the other hand I knew I had to return to my body (lying lifeless below). I know now that I had responsibilities and tasks still to complete on Earth. I had to fulfil my incarnation vows.

Experiencing these two poles, however, did not contradict what I had learnt about there being no dualities. This was because I realized that it was indeed a "both/and". It was possible because I now had an understanding about being the Whole and the One and about just "be-ing" – living in each precious moment (without past or future). By having this understanding, I realized I would be able to do my incarnation tasks with insight and intentionality, creativity and power, because I would be channelling the Divine-Energy. What I now call the Holy Spirit.

The tugging therefore presented me with a choice. Although I was free to stay where I was, which I very much wanted to do, the purpose of the communication was for me to return to my body and "be" on Earth to complete my work. I now realized that this work was "a healing ministry". All my previous training as a health professional had been preparation for this new orientation and task. I now had to begin it more fully and creatively. I also had to do it by just "be-ing". I had to *be* that Love that I am, manifesting compassion, peace and joy in everything that I would do in the future (although there is no past or future but only each here-and-now). Having a choice meant that I became aware of how, it is only when I am in my true-essence, I can "know" what to decide.

So the tugging confirmed the "real-me", that healthily integrated and strong being who is capable of being intentioned – willing and witting. I "knew" that in returning to Earth, I would still be in the Whole and would be fulfilling my incarnation's meaning and purpose to become a healer. So, suddenly I was back in my body.

Elizabeth M Angas

James Gordon has a major interest in synchronicity, based in personal experience, which curiously seems to have spread to friends and family, and even to his students. He has recently published two books on the subject, Ravens in Full Bloom *and* The Greek Class, *both available from Amazon, along with now ten other books.*

My mother, a strict Catholic on the surface, visited mediums when I was young, less so as I grew older. I remember her telling fortunes at a school fête, using an ordinary pack of cards. She looked the part. At the College where she taught she was nicknamed the Gypsy Queen.

She died in 1970. I continued to live in her house, but shared it with three friends. One of them, a youth worker, invited four teenage girls back – on a 'planned skive' from school. Returning from a meeting, I found the windows and door heavily curtained. I could dimly make out four girls sitting at a table in the front room. It was a séance, and they claimed to have contacted my mother.

Firmly agnostic at the time, I looked on, at first only mildly intrigued. I noted the mistakes. The glass in the centre (each of the girls had their forefinger on it) kept spelling out New York as 'New Yok', in questions about my father. This was indeed where my father lived, not something the girls could have known. At one point I asked the spirit if it 'saw' various people I alone knew, some dead, some still alive. The answers were right in every case. Though errors continued, I ended up 80% convinced.

In 1995 my wife's father died. Soon after, when shopping, a woman approached her. The elderly man she was seeing at her elbow, was he her father? My wife finally went to her for a reading.

Her most impressive insights were about myself. I was currently unemployed, but would get another job in the next six months. I had resigned, and could not rely on references, so this was unexpected. It would be temporary, not at my proper level. I would soon be back up there, but I had to go out and look for it, it wouldn't come to me.

Four months after, a caseworker job was advertised. Despite misgivings, I applied and was short-listed. The bus to the interview was stuck in traffic. On a strong impulse, I got off and started to walk, though I knew I would be at least ten minutes late. I walked past stagnant traffic to find the previous interview had overrun. I got the job. It was temporary, but led to a more permanent post at the "proper level".

As for my wife, the medium correctly predicted she would be a successful therapist, made accurate observations about her father, mother and grandmother, and all three of our sons, one of whom she said was keen on travel. He had recently spent more than a year travelling in the east and on to Australia.

In January 2000 my wife Anne's mother died. Anne consulted a different medium, whose results were so impressive (though mostly relating to Anne's *father*) that I completed a 15-page transcript, from which the passage below is drawn:

... He *knows you are his daughter*... and the feeling of... *not doing his duty*... he feels he *has to pay back*, he has to give you the energy and the love and the feeling of security... (words to the effect: "he did not in his earthly existence")

He's making me believe you have the *potential to earn*... through your own life's experiences you could be a *very good counsellor*... and if you could just get *these studies* under your belt you can get a few *diplomas*... it's a question of... going back and getting certain *certificates* from certain organisations... He knows you are fascinated with tiny bottles...

He's *left some moneys to you or some property* to you, yeah?... has it been... is it *in another country*, or another part of the country? (Anne: "France...") I kept seeing the difficulty as such... but the *worry of it and the actual demands of it*... you've got to sort all that out...

Your father... he went quickly to spirit, he went *suddenly* to spirit, he's saying... but he's saying *after a long illness*... *He knew he was gonna die*, so he thought to himself I will get things sorted... (but)... it's made a complete muddle or a little bit of *unhappiness or... dismay...* with some of the people around you... it could be *brothers and sisters, or stepbrothers and sisters...* I kept feeling his *sharp hurtful words* as if on the earth he *didn't want to know you or he didn't make any attempt to know you...*

He's regretting that now because we all believe in the spiritual philosophy that when we go over to spirit, after compassion and healing has been given and you are ready to look at yourself ... warts and all ... he felt a bit wretched that he *never provided you and Mum with a maintenance or with any moneys to bring you up*. Now he's trying to catch up on giving you back *moneys, property* so you have a better life...

Everything in the above is accurate. The bits I have put in italics are more than just accurate. They could not have been known, or even guessed. This medium knew *absolutely nothing* about Anne from natural sources. Anne had rung up and booked an appointment out of nowhere.

In his last days Anne's father had not allowed her to see him, all the more hurtful as he did allow our sister-in-law to do so. Three times the medium expressed things in French idiom, once in a French accent. Anne did reveal there was a house in France, but she herself does not appear French. She speaks fluent English with no trace of an accent. Plenty of English people have houses in France.

The few inaccuracies were corrected - by the medium herself. 'He went suddenly to spirit' was followed by 'after a long illness'. Neither was wrong. He had been ill for some time, yet his actual death was sudden and unexpected.

The lack of support ('not doing his duty') was all too accurate. He never made any maintenance payments, easier to get away with in France than here. Hardly fruitful territory for a fraudulent medium to guess at, let alone do so accurately.

He volunteered advice on business matters. This was his strongest suit. He had been a successful business man, a multi-millionaire. Nor could the medium have known that my wife was a trained counsellor, that she would a year or so later be practising as an alternative therapist. Her work involves dispensing flower formula pillules in tiny bottles!

Finally, my diary account of a phone-call received, out of the blue, from Jane, a medium friend, a former neighbour, now moved from London. Bette, Anne's mother, had died the week before:

Jane rang ... saying Bette had 'come in' and was showing her pink fingers (no longer stained by nicotine); she was standing in a field and pointing to a blade of grass. In life Bette often referred to a blade of grass in the way that some have referred to the grain of sand in which the whole universe is contained.

A month later Jane rang again. Bette was with her. She had some 'cheap flowers' in one hand, with white petals and a yellow centre; in the other she held a pink pig. Did Anne know what she was on about? Yes, said Anne, coming through from the telephone desk to the kitchen, where I was working at the table. On it was a cluster of large artificial daisies, and a pink wooden pig, used as a letter-sorter. Neither was even visible from where Anne was sitting, and there was no reason for them to be in her mind. (Some believe mediums operate by reading the client's mind.)

Soon after Jane was describing a pen, brown/beige, marbly with a silver top, squareish in design. As they were speaking, Anne produced it from the bottom of her handbag. Bette had never seen this pen in life, any more than Jane had. As with the daisy and the pig, it had been neither in Anne's hand, or her sight, at the time.

I do now fully believe such messages can be sent. Though some such claims may be fraudulent, not all are. I also believe that because a medium makes some mistakes, it does not necessarily invalidate other aspects of their reading.

Edited extract from Chapter 33 of Cedar Bug Boards *by James Gordon.*

James Gordon

6. EXPERIENCES OF EARLY QUAKERS

The truest end of life, is to know the life that never ends. He that makes this his care, will find it his crown at last. And he that lives to live ever, never fears dying; nor can the means be terrible to him that heartily believes the end.

For though death be a dark passage, it leads to immortality, and that's recompense enough for suffering of it. And yet, faith lights us, even through the grave, being the evidence of things not seen.

And this is the comfort of the good, that the grave cannot hold them, and that they live as soon as they die. For death is no more than a turning of us over from time to eternity. Death, then, being the way and condition of life, we cannot love to live, if we cannot bear to die.

They that love beyond the world cannot be separated by it. Death cannot kill what never dies. Nor can spirits ever be divided that love and live in the same Divine Principle, the root and record of their friendship. If absence be not death, neither is theirs.

Death is but crossing the world, as friends do the seas; they live in one another still. For they must needs be present, that love and live in that which is omnipresent. In this divine glass, they see face to face; and their converse is free, as well as pure.

This is the comfort of friends, that though they may be said to die, yet their friendship and society are, in the best sense, ever present, because immortal.

William Penn, 1693

(Quaker Faith and Practice 22.95)

Historian, David Britton, has given immense service to the Fellowship over the years through his study of the relevant writings of the early Quakers. His researches clearly show that for these seventeenth century Friends the physical world was held within and underpinned by a spiritual or heavenly world of far greater significance. A study of the writings from these times reveals how far the Society of the present day has moved from this original belief.

George Fox and the Next World – *extract from a talk given to a QFAS conference by David Britton.*

Without my reading the lengthy *Doctrinals* of Fox, but relying on the various *Narrative Papers of Fox*, edited by Henry Cadbury, *The Book of Miracles*, and other materials of that kind, together with a few crucial passages from the Journal, I find the evidence is that Fox simply took the next world for granted. It was not an issue on which he dissented from the other Christian Churches, except in the manner of its operation, through the terrible principle of predestination, which he rejected.

At the other end of the spectrum, where the radical spirituality of the Ranters wanted to overthrow all notion of an after-life, and to celebrate only its own rather manic here-and-now spirituality, Fox, like Margaret Fell, and Barclay, and Nayler, and several other early 'weighty Quakers', was very firm, and indeed very sharp in condemnation. I have read everything I could lay hands on written by early Quakers on the Ranters, and I can assure you that they speak with one voice.

Here, from *The Narrative Papers*, and quoted by Cecil Sharman in his excellent book *George Fox and the Quakers*, is the story of Margaret Rous and her child – 'Hearing that Margaret Rous' child was sick I went to see it, and as I stood by it considering its condition, I felt the Lord's power go through it, and the word was, the Lord's power was come to raise it up or fetch it away, and so I came away fresh in the Lord's power and satisfied in myself. And the next day her mother came to the town and desired me to go with her to see it, and through her tenderness I went, though I was satisfied in myself. And so I saw the child was full of the power of the Lord, and it rested upon it and rested in it. And at night it died, and afterwards the spirit of the child appeared to me, and there was a mighty substance of glorious life in that child, and I bid her mother be content, for it was well.' Now what could be a clearer statement than that?

George Fox's mother died in 1674, when Fox was in Worcester gaol, and was prevented from visiting her. When the letter about her death reached him, he was grieved, but – 'When my spirit had gotten through I saw her in the resurrection and the life, everlastingly with me, and father in the flesh also' (*Book of Miracles*). Again, could anything be clearer or more whole-hearted?

Here is Fox's Epistle concerning Josiah Cole. '... and Friends sate about him, and healed him, and I went to him, and healed him, and he was full of the power of the Lord, and his seed and Life, that was over all; and so in that he departed away in the arms of Friends, as he sate on the side of his bed, and had a very easy passage through the Life in which he remains.'

Here is part of Fox's Testimony to George Watt. 'And, as Christ saith, He that believeth in me, though he were dead, yet shall he live... in this belief, and in this Life, is our dear brother George Watt; I do see him and feel him.'

And here is another Testimony, this time to Edward Burroughs. 'Dear Edward Burroughs fell asleep on the 14th day of the 12th month 1662, who is with the Lord forever. And that which I eternally loved in him never dies, but lives forever, and so cannot be separated from him.'

And here, as an example of his healing ministry, is his letter in 1658 to Lady Claypole, suffering mental distress – 'For looking down at sin and corruption and distraction, you are swallowed up in it; but looking at the Light that discovers them, you will see over them. That will give victory, and you will find grace and strength, and there is the first step of peace, that will bring salvation, and see to the beginning and the glory that was with the Father before the world began, and so come to know the seed of God which is heir of the promise of God, and the world which hath no end unto the power of an endless life, which power of God is immortal, which brings up the Soul which is immortal, up to the immortal God, in whom it doth rejoice.'

That, making all due allowance for Fox's puzzling (yet powerful) cumulative style of writing, is also a clear statement of the immortality of the Soul at the highest level, in God himself.

A tribute at a similar high level is given in Fox's Testimony to the truly great Isaac Penington, in 1679. 'And he did freely minister of his living bread and water, which he had received from above, from the living God and his Son, to the comfort of them that feared the Lord, and kept their habitation in the Truth, in meekness and humility. And I do know that he is well in the Lord, and in Peace with him through the Lord Jesus Christ'.

Some Quakers have said to me that an eventual resurrection in the body is the true voice of Christianity, not the life of the Soul immediately after death, in a Soul-world. To present such a stark opposition of ideas is unnecessary, and even false. Both ideas might be true. Or another alternative, seemingly favoured by Fox, and by some of today's psychical researchers, is that a form of bodily existence is the immediate reality of the next world, together with the Soul. Whichever principle we adopt as our belief, the crucial point encompassed by all these positions, is that our physical death is not the end of our story, and to this principle Fox and the early Quakers remained faithful.

Margaret Fell and the Next World – extract from a *talk given to a QFAS conference by David Britton*

Margaret Fell, as we hardly need reminding, was one of the truly great founders of Quakerism. Her warmth and broad humanity reach us today, where the over-refining of Quaker culture in later periods can leave us feeling a little chilly. Her acute spiritual discernment was vital to the early movement, as was the "Liberty Hall" of her family home at Swarthmoor, a place of refuge during the years of persecution, and also a kind of secretariat for the Society.

Margaret Fell's confidence about the heavenly world is shown in several places in her writings, but in none more impressively than her Testimony to her second husband, George Fox, on his death in 1691. (She outlived him by 11 years). Here she said: "It has pleased God to take away my dear husband out of this evil troublesome world, who was not a man thereof, being chosen out of it, and had his life and being in another region... so I am now to give my account and testimony for my dear husband, whom the Lord has taken unto His blessed kingdom and glory... Now he has finished his course and his testimony, and is entered into his eternal rest and felicity."

On another note is Margaret's dialogue with a Ranter. The Ranter says: "What pre-eminence hath a man above a beast?" Margaret replies: "*Thou art as the beast which perish* ...Thou knows not the spirit of a man that goes upwards ... thy portion is with the beasts of the field... "

In her 1656 Epistle to Meetings she talks of Christ giving "eternal life" to "his sheep". Many modern Friends will of course say that eternal life is lived only in the here and now but this is not what early Friends believed, as is shown by Margaret Fell's 1659 "Pastoral Letter to certain Friends" in which she writes: "the Spirit of the Saints in light savours the eternal life in all, and loves it in all, and sees and feels it in all." She is here referring to the departed spirits of "the Saints", and she goes on to say: "... And so here is the resting place that you must all meet in where the true fellowship is one with another, which all the Saints in light was gathered into since the

beginning, and all meets here from Eternity to Eternity...".
And if there should be any doubt about her meaning, here is a passage from her 1656 "Epistle to Friends" – "Therefore, if you love your Soul, which is immortal, abide in the Light and live the Light and walk in the Light, where the Fellowship and the Unity is."

In an interesting letter to the Jews in 1656, sent to Spinoza in Amsterdam, she writes, "Our soul's desire is that you might be gathered and come into the Covenant of Light and partake with us of the everlasting riches and inheritance that never fades away."

Many things point compellingly towards an experience of what Anglicans and Catholics and Orthodox celebrate as their Communion of Saints. For early Quakers it was clearly a vivid reality, not least because of the many Quaker martyrs in that first generation. The presence of the departed in those early Meetings must have been very important, a comfort and an inspiration for those struggling against persecution on earth. This is something that has been neglected in Quaker historical studies. And what a loss it is to Quakerism that those living presences are no longer welcomed in Meeting for Worship or elsewhere. An openness to them would transform our Society.

Here are decisive passages from the Testimony of her children to Margaret Fell after her death in 1702: "And the blessed God of Heaven and Earth preserved her in a good understanding to the last... and we believe she is inheriting a Heavenly Mansion, prepared by the Lord Jesus Christ, for all His faithful followers."

Even more telling is the Testimony of George Whitehead, in that it clearly reveals the sophisticated early Quaker understanding of the relation between eternal life on earth and eternal life in heaven: "She retained a sincere and constant love to all faithful Friends and brethren to the end, which was a true evidence of her being passed from death to life *while here,* [my emphasis] and her portion in eternal life and felicity in the heavenly kingdom..."

A phrase such as "passing from death to life" while on earth is of course eagerly seized on by modern "spiritual" Quakers as proof that the early Quakers saw no need for life after death.

In support of this there is a passage from Thomas Camm's Testimony to her: "… and now she is rewarded with the *full fruition* [my emphasis] of eternal life and Peace with her God."

Passages from Pendle Hill Pamphlet 340, A Quaker Way of Dying, *by Lucy McIver. Selected by David Britton.*

… For early Quakers the inevitability of death was not denied, but directly addressed. In the manner of a clearness committee, family members of Quaker elders would ask questions to help the dying discern the clarity of their spiritual condition. Accordingly, they were encouraged to surrender and accept God's will. Such spiritual support is apparent in William Penn's counsel to his son, Springette, who died at age 21. Before his illness Springette had desired to travel in the ministry with his father. Penn addressed his son's grief of letting go of this hope by saying:

'My dear child, if it please the Lord to raise thee, I am satisfied it will be so; and if not, then in as much as it is thy fervent desire in the Lord, he will look upon thee just as if thou didst live to serve him, and thy comfort will be the same. So, either way, it will be well; for if thou shouldst not live, I do verily believe thou wilt have the recompense of thy good desires, without the temptations and troubles that would attend if long life were granted to thee.'

And Springette surrendered his desire and replied to his father: 'My eye looks another way, where the truest pleasure is … All is mercy, dear father; everything is mercy.

"In spiritual counsel and within the support of gathered worship, the pain of illness and letting go of this physical life was vicariously shared by all in attendance to the dying. The gifts of ministry would reciprocally flow to all in the death chamber. As the dying person surrendered to God's will, he or she would ask family or friends likewise to surrender. The one who was dying would often minister to the family acknowledging their shared grief, reminding them to trust in God and accept God's will in their dying. This was a request built upon a foundation of faith."

The death of my mentor and friend, Teresina Havens, strongly witnesses this joyful faith. Being 84 years old and diagnosed with congestive heart failure, she *knew* her time for dying was at hand. She prepared for death with great anticipation. Shortly before her transition she dreamed that while studying at school the intercom announced – "*Teresina Havens is graduating.*" With joy and a sense of release she planned her rites of passage calling close friends and family together to celebrate her birth into largeness.

Teresina lived her dying labour with joy. She surrendered her self-will to a sense of fullness and believed fully that as her physical body diminished an inner part of her would join a Divine order. It was a faith in the wholeness of life and death. She had found the promise of this in the dying words of a seventeenth century Friend, Richard Hubberthorne, and requested that this ministry be read as a statement of her faith during her rites of passage:

> *'This night or tomorrow night*
> *I shall depart hence …*
> *Do not seek to hold me*
> *For it is too strait for me;*
> *And out of this straitness I must go,*
> *For I am wound into largeness.…'*

When death appeared and said, 'it's time to die,'
I, having all my life my God denied,
Began to wonder who would be the I
Who lived forever on the other side.

Had I been so selfish all my days
That my True Self I'd always failed to show?
I never thought to sing God's praise,
How, after death, would I my True Self know?

Then, in perplexity, at last I died;
And O what comfort, Friends, it was to see
The one I found upon the other side
Was still the person I had felt was me.

Now, beyond all Time, I realise
I'm smaller than I thought, up Here above,
But gone are all my vanities and lies
And what is left (Praise Be!) is Holy Love.

So, when I'm born again with choice
Of being less selfish, my True Love to prove,
I know I'll listen to that small Voice,
Which says, 'If you'd be me, be Holy Love!'

John Hemming, a Quaker poet.
He used to receive his poems during his sleep at night.
He would wake up with a fully formed poem in his head.

SUGGESTIONS FOR FURTHER READING

Booklist

Many of the older books listed have stood the test of time, become classics and been reprinted. Their present state of availability may be seen on the internet.

Many of the writers of more recent books also have websites with links to interviews and lectures, etc.

Alexander, Eben, *Proof of Heaven*, Piatkus, 2012, *The Map of Heaven*, 2014, *Living in a Mindful Universe*, 2017.

Atwater, PMH, *The Big book of Near-Death experiences*, Rainbow Ridge, 2014.

Bailey, Lee and Yates, Jenny (editors), *The Near-Death experience, a Reader*, Routledge, 1996.

Barbanell, Sylvia, *When your child dies*, Psychic Press, 1942. *When Your Animal Dies*, Psychic Press, 1942.

Beard, Paul, *Survival of Death*, 1966. *Living On*, 1980. *Hidden Man*, 1986, Pilgrim Books.

Bloom, William, *The Endorphin Effect: A breakthrough strategy for holistic and spiritual wellbeing*, Piatkus, 2001.

Cadbury, Henry J., *George Fox's Book of Miracles*, Cambridge University Press, 1948.

Conan Doyle, Arthur, *History of Spiritualism* (2 volumes), pub. 1926.

Cummins, Geraldine, *Swan on a Black Sea*, Routledge & Kegan Paul, 1965.

Dossey, Larry, *One Mind*, 2013. (Other titles).

Dowding, Lord, *Many Mansions*, 1943. *Lychgate*, 1945.

Fenwick, Peter & Elizabeth, *The Art of Dying*, Continuum, 2008.

Findlay, Arthur, *The Rock of Truth*, Psychic Press, 1933. (Other titles).

Fontana, David, *Is There an Afterlife? A Comprehensive Overview of the Evidence*, O-Books, 2005. *Life Beyond Death: What Should We Expect?*, Watkins, 2009.

Fuller, John, *The Airmen Who Would Not Die*, 1979.

Galloway, Donald, *Inevitable Journey*, Con-Psy Publications, 1994.

Graff, Dale E., *Tracks in the Psychic Wilderness: An exploration of remote viewing, ESP, pre-cognition, dreaming and synchronicity*, Element, 1998.

Greaves, Helen, *Testimony of Light*, World Fellowship Press for the Churches' Fellowship for Psychical and Spiritual Studies, 1969.

Heathcote-James, Emma, *They Walk Among Us: After Death Communication*, John Blake Publishing, 2004.

Hodges, David, *George Fox and the Healing Ministry*. Pub. Friends' Fellowship of Healing. 1995. *Do We Survive Death? A descriptive bibliography on the evidence supporting survival*, 2004.

Howard, Angela, *Only a Thought Away*, Quacks Books, 2010.

Kübler-Ross, Elisabeth, *On Life After Death*, Celestial Arts, 1991. (Other titles.)

Lambillion, Paul, *Auras and Colours – A Guide to Subtle Energies*, Gateway/Gill & MacMillan, 2003. (Other titles.)

Lehmann, Rosamund, *The Swan in the Evening. Fragments of an inner life*, Collins, 1967. *The Awakening Letters* (co-author Cynthia Sandys), Neville Spearman, 1978.

Lodge, Oliver, *Raymond Revised: A new and abbreviated edition of Raymond or Life After Death with an additional chapter*, Methuen & Co., 1922.

Manning, Matthew, *The Link*, Colin Smythe Ltd (new edition), 1987.

Mason, Don, *Science Mystical Experience and Religious Truth*, Sessions, 2006.

McIver, Lucy Screechfield, *Pendle Hill pamphlet 340, The Quaker Way of Dying*.

McTaggart, Lynne, *The Field: The quest for the secret force of the universe*, Element, 2003. (Other titles.)

Moody, Raymond, *Life After Life*, Mockingbird Books, 1975. (Other titles include *Glimpses of Beyond* and *The Light Beyond*.)

Moorjani, Anita, *Dying to be me*, Hay House Publishing, 2012.

Muldoon, Sylvan, *Projection of the Astral Body*, Muller Press (reprint) 2011.

Myers, F.W.H., *Human Personality and its Survival of Bodily Death*, Longmans Green, 1903. An abridged version appeared in 1919.

Newton, Michael, *Journey of Souls* (case studies of life between lives) and other titles, Llewellyn Publications, 1994.

Northage, Ivy, *Mediumship Made Simple*, Psychic Press, 1986.

Parnia, Sam, What *Happens when We Die?*, Hay House, 2007.

Polge, Coral, *Living Images: The Story of a Psychic Artist*, Regency Press, 1985 and the Spiritualist Association of Great Britain, 1997.

Rose, Aubrey, *Journey into Immortality*. Lennard Publishing. 1997.

Sartori, Penny, *The Wisdom of Near Death Experiences: how NDEs can help us to live more fully*, 2014. (Other titles.)

Sheldrake, Rupert, *A New Science of Life: The Hypothesis of Morphic Resonance*, J. P. Tarcher, 1981. (Other titles.)

Sheridan, Kim, *Animals and the Afterlife*, Hay House, 2003

Sherwood, Jane, *The Country Beyond*, Neville Spearman Ltd, 1944. *Post-Mortem Journal*, Neville Spearman Ltd, 1964. *The Four-Fold Vision*, Neville Spearman Ltd, 1965. Edition combining *The Psychic Bridge and The Country Beyond*, 1969. *Peter's Gate: a Book for the Elderly*, CFPSS, 1973.

Shine, Betty, *Mind to Mind*, Bantam Books, 1991. Also *Mind Magic, Mind Waves* and *Betty Shine's workbook*. Pub. Corgi.

Simpkin, Cherry, *The Forest of Now: A Spiritual Allegory*, Hazelnut Books, 2014. 78 Courtlands Ave, Lee, London, SE12 8JA.

Smith, Rosalind, *Quakers and the Spiritual/Psychic Dimension*. Available from Friends Fellowship of Healing: The Manager, Claridge House, Dormansland, Lingfield, Surrey, RH7 6QH.

Straughan, Roger, *A Study in Survival: Conan Doyle Solves the Final Problem*, O-Books, 2009.

Sudman, Natalie, *Application of Impossible Things*, Ozark Mountain Publishing, 2012.

Tudor Pole, Wellesley, *Private Dowding, 1917*. (Other titles).

Tymn, Michael, *Dead Men Talking: Afterlife Communication from WW1*, White Crow Books, 2014.

Walsch, Neale Donald, *The New Revelations: A Conversation with God*. Hodder and Stoughton, 2003.

Wambach, Helen, *Reliving Past Lives*, Hutchinson, 1979.

Watson, Lyall, *The Romeo Error*, Hodder and Stoughton, 1980.

Weiss, Brian, *Many Lives, Many Masters*, Piatkus Books, 1994. (Other titles).

Van Lommel, Pim & Hines-Woollacot, Marjorie, *Infinite Awareness: The Awakening of a Scientific Mind*, Rowman & Littlefield, 2018. (Other titles).

Zammit, Victor & Wendy, *A Lawyer Presents the Evidence for the Afterlife*, White Crow Books, 2013.

Channelled books

Cummins, Geraldine, *The Road to Immortality. Being a description of the After-life purporting to be communicated by the late F.W.H Myers*, Ivor Nicholson & Watson Ltd., 1933.

The Findhorn Foundation. There are many books published by Findhorn Publications, The Park, Forres, 1V36 0TZ, Scotland. Among them are two booklets *The Living Word* and *Footprints on the Path* by Eileen Caddy. www.Findhorn.org

Lambillion, Paul, *Communications from Heartstar*, L.N. Fowler & Co Ltd. 1993.

Rodegast, Pat and Judith Stanton (compilers), *Emmanuel's Book: A manual for living comfortably in the cosmos*, 1987. *Emmanuel's Book II: The choice for love*, Bantam Books, 1989.

White, Ruth, *Gildas Communicates, Seven Inner Journeys, The Healing Spectrum, A Question of Guidance*. C.W. Daniel.

Winkworth, Eileen. *More Truth communicated by Arthur Findlay*, Harmony Press, 1985.

Organisations

The Arthur Findlay College, Stansted Hall, Stansted, Essex, CM24 8UD. www.snu.org.uk Phone 01279-813636.

The Churches Fellowship for Psychical and Spiritual Studies, Office 8, The Creative Suite, Mill 3, Pleasley Vale Business Park, Mansfield, Nottinghamshire NG19 8RL www.churchesfellowship.org.uk
Phone. 01623 812206.

CRUSE. www.Crusebeareavementcare.org.uk.

The Leslie Flint Educational Trust, 13 Pembridge Place, London, W2 4XB. www.leslieflint.com Email. info@leslieflint.com

IANDS The International Association for Near Death Studies (website.)

Society for Psychical Research, 49 Marloes Rd, London, W8 6LA. www.spr.ac.uk

The College of Psychic Studies, 16 Queensberry Place, London, SW7 2EB. www.collegeofpsychicstudies.co.uk. Phone: 020-7589-3292/3.

The Spiritualist Association of Great Britain, 33 Belgrave Square, London, SW1X 8QB. www.sagb.org.uk Phone: 020-7235-3351.

The Unitarian Society for Psychical Studies
www.ukunitarians.org.uk/psychical Secretary, David Taylor, infousps@yahoo.com

White Eagle Lodge, New Lands, Liss, Hampshire, GU33 7HY. There are many books published by The White Eagle Publishing Trust. 15 booklets of White Eagle's teachings. www.whiteagle.org. Journal, Stella Polaris.